...main

Rose Trem... ...r novels:
SADLER'... ...RD, THE
SWIMMING POOL SEASON, RESTORATION, which
won the *Sunday Express* Book of the Year Award in 1989,
was shortlisted for the Booker Prize and has recently
been made into a major film, and SACRED COUNTRY,
which won th... 1993 James Tait Black Memorial Prize
and the... ...s also
written three vol... ...NEL'S
DAUGHTER, which won the Dylan Thomas Short
Story Award in 1984, THE GARDEN OF THE VILLA
MOLLINI, and EVANGELISTA'S FAN. She has written
numerous plays for radio and television, including
TEMPORARY SHELTER, winner of a Giles Cooper Award.
Rose Tremain lives in Norfolk and London with the
biographer, Richard Holmes.

Also by Rose Tremain and published by Sceptre

The Colonel's Daughter and Other Stories
The Cupboard
The Garden of the Villa Mollini
Restoration
Sacred Country
Sadler's Birthday
The Swimming Pool Season

Letter to
Sister
Benedicta

ROSE TREMAIN

SCEPTRE

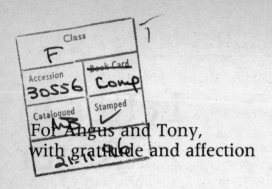

For Angus and Tony,
with gratitude and affection

First published in Great Britain in 1989 by Hamish Hamilton Ltd.
First published in paperback in 1990 by Hodder and Stoughton
A division of Hodder Headline PLC
A Sceptre Paperback

10 9 8 7 6 5 4

A CIP catalogue record for this book is
available from the British Library

ISBN 0 340 53047 2

Printed and bound in Great Britain by
Cox and Wyman Ltd, Reading, Berkshire

Hodder and Stoughton
A division of Hodder Headline PLC
338 Euston Road
London NW1 3BH

DECEMBER 6 1977

I was there at the beginning. Mother of Noel and Alexandra, wife of Leon. I was there in London last year in December with a grey Christmas on my mind, spending money and waiting, spending time with myself. The window-sills of the flat, I noticed, seemed to be rotting away. The weight of all the wet London mornings was slowly rotting them to nothing and I said to Leon, "Have you noticed this rot everywhere creeping right to our windows?" I said, "Have you noticed the ironwork on the balcony, so sore with its blisters of rust that one can't bear to touch it?" This was when it began, Sister. I shall try to say it all to you, Sister Benedicta, whom I imagine still in the hot courtyard of the Convent School in India, tiny nun in grey when I was a fat girl.

I've begun going to church again. I walk to the Brompton Oratory and in all its vastness whisper a little puff of prayer for Leon who lies in the hospital with tubes up his nose and a bag out of his stomach and who can't make a sound any more but has to write down the few things that cross his mind on a little slate. "The night nurse masturbates" he wrote the first time he wrote anything down and a few days later, the second time he reached for the slate, he tried to write this again but his hand was very feeble that day and all he could write was "the night nurse m". But I take hope, Sister, from this and from the other little things he's written since writing that and have got into the habit of asking God to spare him. If you were here, Sister Benedicta, I would ask you to ask God to spare him even though he's a Jew and thinks that nuns are the carrion of the world. We could kneel down side by side in the bathroom – I've never prayed anywhere but the bathroom since I married Leon – and say something out loud to God and to the repeating kingfishers on the wallpaper. You would pray with your white hands folded under your breasts and I would pray in the manner of someone learning to pray, doing a kind of prayer exercise with

5

my fists pushed into my eyes. We could ask God to give Leon back.

I was quite wrong to imply that Leon has written several things on his slate. He's only written three things altogether since he became conscious. He wrote "the night nurse masturbates", then on the day his hand seemed very weak like an old man's hand he wrote "the night nurse m" and after that he wrote nothing for three days until one morning when I went to visit him and he suddenly picked up the slate and wrote "the aforementioned Richard Mayhew Wainwright" and I honestly couldn't tell you what this means or whether it's a good sign or a bad. Sometimes it seems to me that if he can write long words like "aforementioned" and "masturbate" and spell them correctly he must be getting better, but who can say? Not the doctors. They don't utter a sentence in the way of comfort or hope. They are extremely gentle with me, the doctors, never rude or cross, but I long for them to utter and they don't. They say, "It's really too early to tell, Mrs Constad. You must be patient."

I remember the way it rained in India, Sister. You, the nuns, would turn on all the lights in the classrooms and in the corridors and though you often said you couldn't bear the terrible heat of India you went mute with the rains, thinking of Noah and great floods and disasters in your silence. The day the Viceroy visited the Convent School the rains broke and we heard their drumming in the middle of our "welcome" pageant and wondered about the Viceroy's plumes and the Viceroy's wife in her finery as we made the word "welcome" in girls across the dais. I was one half of the "o" in "welcome", arching forward, feet and fingertips pressed to another girl who was the other half of the "o" and I could smell her menstrual blood as we arched and stretched for the Viceroy and I thought, Lord I hope she doesn't bleed onto the dais in front of the Viceroy's wife who looks so fine and beautiful in her silk dress that you couldn't imagine blood ever flowing out of her.

6

Leon is quite bloodless in the private room, no wound anywhere, nothing to see except the changes in him that are so hard to describe. When I look at him, I imagine the smallness of his heart with its branching arteries and veins compared to the whole size of him and then I marvel that it still keeps him going. I talk to him; I jabber away. I don't tell him that I go to the Oratory and pay 10p for a candle to stop his spirit flickering out; I don't say, I'm imagining your heart, Leon, so small inside the rest of you and can't believe that it will ever let you run, dear, even talk, because your face under the tubes seems so absolutely blank and only the right side of you moves under your blankets, but I talk about the weather and the difficulty of getting taxis and the price of flowers and about the men who have come to repaint the window-sills so that they'll stop rotting away in the damp and fumes and "when you come home, Leon," I say, "you'll find all the window-sills done and as good as new." I never talk to him about Alexandra and Noel. I think he wants to forget about them and I must not interrupt this forgetting in case it helps to make him well. But quite often I want to shout out: "I was there at the beginning of it all, Leon. I saw it happen and there is no need to lie down and die because of it. Look at me, fat still, fifty-year-old woman with a crocodile handbag who last week had a cry in the powder room at Harrods, but not *dying*, Leon, not dying, Sister Benedicta, silent nun dead or alive wherever you are . . ."

Fat, curly-haired girl, Ruby Waterhouse, with my red cheeks and big thighs like my father's so that his uniform always looked stretched and my mother often laughed: "Don't split your breeches, Harry, on parade!" I haven't often given her a thought, so preoccupied, you see, with the comings and goings of my family for twenty-six years, trying to care for Leon, proud of the way he's kept his body in trim, there really hasn't been time to remember the Convent School and the funny ways of the English in India, trying so hard to make everything just like Wiltshire with picnics and tennis parties.

7

But I do remember her now and then, just as now and then I've taken to walking to the Oratory and doing my poor prayer and coming out again wondering, could that have done any good? And if I see myself reflected in Harrods' windows (sometimes I walk straight by the windows, not looking at the display, afraid for some reason to see a reflection) I think, Ruby Constad that's all you've got, only the self that was once Ruby Waterhouse, daughter of a Colonel with my big thighs and my bad deportment and then I feel my thighs rubbing together as I walk and the touch of my own warm skin is comforting: I can go on.

It rained the day that Noel didn't come home. We thought he'd be catching the 10.30 from Cambridge and Leon said "boil a chicken for lunch" and I said "boilers are very hard to find these days, Leon." But I walked to the butchers in my green mac and got a boiler and on the way home bought some dyed teasels from a drenched barrow boy who said "Happy Christmas, lady" and I thought, oh Lord, only ten days and we'll be eating plum pudding. My stomach felt uncomfortable from all the eating we'd done the evening before at Betty Hazlehurst's dinner party, eating and eating and getting hot in my mauve cocktail dress but trying to listen to Gerald Tibbs, the man on my left, pale man with little shivering hands who couldn't eat a thing, he said, since his wife had left him, left him and gone off with a smart-alec Romeo, left him alone in the house with all her things, even her furs and gilt-framed pictures of the children. "She'll come back," I said to the pale man, Gerald, idiotic thing to say when of course she won't.

> She's gone to Milan
> with her smart young man
> leaving her furs
> and all that was hers
> including the very
> pale man she called Gerry.

"I'm so sorry," I said, "I didn't mean to say 'she'll come back'. What a stupid thing to say when of course she may not.

8

The thing is, these kind of social occasions seem to take away . . ."

"What?" said Gerald Tibbs.

"Compassion." I said.

So the next day, as it rained on London and I noticed the window-sills for the first time, Leon came home for lunch to welcome Noel and Noel never arrived. We waited in the drawing-room, Leon staring out beyond the rotting balcony to the street. I mixed us each a martini and laid the table, made a sauce for the chicken and sat down, remembering the kind of noise Noel always made in our flat, wondering why, when he'd been a quiet little boy, he was now so full of shouting and loud laughter. Leon kept looking at his watch. "Do sit down, Leon," I said, but he went on pacing by the window. "Half past one," he said.

At two o'clock we ate a little bit of chicken, but after a few mouthfuls, Leon decided that he felt very tired and went to telephone his office to say he wouldn't be coming back. After he'd telephoned, he flopped down on the sofa in the drawing-room where he fell asleep and his piece of chicken in its sauce went cold and I unwrapped the dyed teasels from their sodden newspaper and stuck them in Grandma Constad's Chinese vase where they stood erect and dead. I crept into the drawing-room with the vase of teasels where Leon sat asleep. I put the vase down without a sound.

It is mortally silent in Leon's room at the nursing home. Most of the time he seems to be in a kind of sleep and isn't aware of me. His clients have sent expensive flowers and his room is a bower. I notice the armchair where the night nurse sits with her hand up her skirt. I wonder if the night nurse is young. I wonder if in the depths of his inert being Leon feels his cock stir for the night nurse. I want to lie down on the bed and hold Leon, but I'm afraid to do this because of the tubes that mustn't be moved and because day nurses come in and out all the time to look at him.

9

Leon, who is a solicitor, has – or used to have – lots of "cases" going on interminably, a constant stream of adulterers for instance seemed to pass through his office, actors and filmstars, never a shortage of them and people who had been libelled demanding money to erase the truth. "I don't know how you can bear it, the constant interminable stream," I once said to Leon, but he laughed and then made a fist and said, "I'm a fighter, Ruby!" But though he enjoys fighting in his office, smartly decorated office with nine and a half paces of brown carpet and his secretary Sheila always alert for his buzzer, he seems quite unwilling to fight for his life, so all I can hope is that "the aforementioned Richard Mayhew Wainwright" is one of the rich and famous and adulterous for whom Leon fights so well and that if this case is on his mind it will give Leon a bit of strength to struggle through. Unless, Sister Benedicta, God notices my 10p candles. But what are the chances when it is so long since I was a good Catholic and said my prayers anywhere but the bathroom?

On the day that Noel never arrived, Leon didn't wake till four. It was dark by four, darker because the rain kept on. I had washed up and then sat opposite Leon in the drawing-room, reading the Margaret Drabble novel lent to me by Alexandra until it became too dark to see a word she'd written and I was afraid to switch on the light, preferring to watch Leon sleep and to sit silently for a while wondering at last what had happened to Noel, for until that moment I hadn't really given him a thought, letting Leon who loved Noel so much worry for the two of us. Now I let myself remember Noel. I imagined him standing in the drawing-room, taller than both Leon and me, his body very pleased with itself, disconcerting in its little boastful ways, a thing to love and fear if you were a girl and twenty, or even if you were me, fat all my life, never imagining myself the mother of a tall son with straight brown hair that flopped and shone and a voice that was too loud.

Leon wants Noel to become a solicitor. "My son," he sometimes says proudly, "is very like me: he has an innate under-standing of the law." Of course it's some days since Leon has said that or anything at all, but that Friday in London when we waited for Noel I knew that Leon was looking forward to him being with us for a while so that when clients came to dinner as they often did he could say those kind of things. But he never asked Noel how he was doing at Cambridge, never wrote to Noel's tutor saying "does my boy have an innate under-standing of the law?" He invented Noel's "innate under-standing of the law" out of love and fear and out of love and fear Noel never contradicted him. I know now – Alexandra told me – that Noel hated the fat books of the law and during the course of that very term at Cambridge had decided to give it up.

So there we waited, the afternoon darkness on us, sitting uselessly together until at four Leon woke and looked at his illuminated watch and seeing the time was quite bewildered, not knowing where he was or why, and called out for me. "Here I am, Leon," I said gently, "I'm going to put on the light."

Leon blinked at me and remembered. "Has Noel come?" he said.

"No, Leon, Noel hasn't come and I was only waiting for you to finish your little sleep to say surely we ought to telephone his landlady?" And when I remember saying this, I can't imagine why one of us, Leon at least, hadn't thought of doing this earlier because had we telephoned at two when Leon flopped down for his sleep we might have spoken to Noel and as it was we didn't telephone till four and a far-away sounding Mrs Walton said: "Oh no, Mrs Constad, Noel's packed and gone." But Leon at once said: "Packed and gone could mean anything. It could simply mean he's catching a later train, Ruby, so why don't you pop out, dear, before the shops shut and get some cakes and things for his tea?" So I put on my green mac and began another of my countless walks up Knightsbridge, knowing as I saw myself pass in all the shop windows that Noel wouldn't be coming for tea, that in his uncaring way he had decided on something else.

Obedience to Leon (why else was I walking up Knightsbridge in the rain for cakes?) comes very easily to me. Leon believes that he is right in his little commands; Leon believes in his own answers. So my obedience to Leon comes I think not from my belief that he's always right, but from his. I don't question. I let Leon be right. I have let other people be right all my life. Yet I have begun lately to wonder at this unfashionable tendency of mine and think it may have something to do with being fat and wish now and then that I lived in seventeenth-century Holland and was a mistress of Rubens and he would joy in my big thighs and paint me laughing and naked and my nipples flamingo pink. Alexandra despises my habit of obedience when in the 1970s she believes that women must say no to everything and go on and on saying no so that men will repent of their arrogance and in the spirit of lambs lie down with the lionesses to draft a new constitution for the Western world and God knows we do need a new constitution because our world has lost count of all its sorrows and people like me have so absolutely lost count of them that no wonder I sometimes feel like a dinosaur who should be dead under the great forests of coal.

There were none of Noel's favourite cakes in Harrods' food halls. I bought one or two Danish things, thinking these might keep better than ordinary cake, knowing Leon and I wouldn't want to eat cakes on our own. But when I came out of Harrods, the rain had passed on and was falling on Highgate or Camden Town or somewhere to the north, sparing Knightsbridge which was unexpectedly gleaming in pale sunlight. So I walked home with my umbrella folded, discovering in the bit of sunshine that I was hurrying, believing suddenly that after all Noel might have arrived and wanting to get home with the cakes and see Leon full of relief and joy. The pavements were very slippery and my left leg almost skidded down a grating and the cakes

12

with it, but my heart was now quite bright with expectation and in all the taxis that passed me I looked for Noel, sure to see him now with his odd Cambridge paraphernalia, happy to see him in spite of his noise and Leon's doting on him, thinking after all he is my son, my first-born child and never mind if there's no peace in the flat for three weeks as long as he's there and I can now and then reach out and touch him.

But the flat was quiet when I got home. No sign of Noel and Leon was sitting where he'd been asleep, staring worriedly at the room. I put the cakes on the kitchen table and thought, they're a waste of money, the cakes, they'll never be eaten.

Then I sat down by Leon and took his neat hand in my podgy one (I remember on my wedding day seeing our hands side by side for the first time and smiling at the difference in them) and said: "We're bound to hear, Leon, sooner or later." Leon nodded. "Thoughtless little sod!" he said, turning away and I nodded, recalling that Leon said "thoughtless little sod" quite often about all sorts of people who arrived late or stayed too long or forgot to deliver his drink order or drove cars in any way inimical to him, and I found it odd that he put the word "little" in there when he himself, though a neat and quite handsome man, only measures five foot eight.

"Noel's not little," I said.

"Little of spirit," he declared, "if he can let his mother down like this!"

I pondered this, remembering how surely Leon had let his own mother down by marrying not merely a gentile but an alleged Catholic and that he had tried all his life until her death in 1970 to atone for this by buying her presents and bits of her favourite Jewish food and by letting her who had been poor all her life and widowed at thirty-one come to see him in his huge office to prove that he hadn't failed her.

"It's not me so much, dear," I said quietly, "as you."

But Leon didn't reply to this, lit one of his small cigars and puffed away at it in silence until it was gone.

13

I haven't mentioned Alexandra, Sister. Alexandra was twenty then. When she was eighteen she left London and her room that seemed still to be a little girl's room and went to an art school in Norwich. Leon bought her a mini. She moved into a cottage near Wymondham with a friend called Sue. "We love the cottage," Alexandra told me, "even though it's cold and Sue says why not keep our own chickens?" So of her life I knew scarcely more than this. "You'd hate the cottage, Mummy," she told me, "so don't come up and see us and anyway it's only got two bedrooms." And obedient even to her, I've never been there, but used to imagine her there in the cottage with her paintings and her friend Sue whom I've never met. I worried about her when really I shouldn't she kept telling me because she'd never been so happy and if ever she felt overtired from all the painting she was doing she'd just go and feed the hens (because of course Sue had bought the hens and a hen coop straight away, no sooner mentioned than there they were free-ranging all over the garden) and listen to their little noises until she felt peaceful again. "So please don't *worry*," she kept saying, "not about me!" And I believe I did try not to think of her, saying to myself, she is quite free.

"We don't have favourites," you used to say, Sister Benedicta, "in this school. You are all God's children and we are here to do God's work." But how then could I have stayed whispering in your room with its narrow bed and raffia blinds on countless late afternoons with sundown coming on, whispering about poetry and all the young poets who were dying of love for somebody, writing of a love they could die for and I had never felt any love except the love of your immaculate quietness, Sister Benedicta, and your little room with the blinds where you made tea. Did *all* the girls come creeping to your room to whisper about Keats? Did they have tea? If you were here now, Sister, when we knelt down by the bath and said our prayers for Leon, I could ask you, "wasn't I your favourite?" And then I wouldn't be afraid to say that it's very hard for me to let Alexandra be free because of my two children I love her so much the best that if Leon's going to die in spite of the candles and the prayers I would want to go and be with her. Quite often I pass on my walks a small shop that sells paraffin stoves and I think to myself, if I took a paraffin stove or even two paraffin stoves to Alexandra's cottage, then all of us would be warm. Not that she'd want me there in her life that she's trying so hard to rearrange. I'd be in her way all the time and in Sue's way and I dare say the hens would stop laying.

The telephone call from Noel came very late on the Friday night when Leon and I were in bed with our bedside lights on and through my spectacles I was peering once again at the Margaret Drabble. Leon has the telephone on his side of the bed in case one of his famous clients – who never seem to go to bed at all or else keep popping over to California where night is day – ring him at two in the morning, just like you might ring a doctor or a Samaritan, believing that Leon is quite happy to talk to them any time, even at sundown in Beverly Hills, which he is. So Leon answered the telephone and kept saying. "Speak up, speak up Noel. I can't hear what you're saying." But then it turned out that what Noel was saying made Leon wish he hadn't heard it because I put down the Margaret Drabble and watched Leon and his face did, in the manner of a stage direction I once read, "register extreme disappointment" so that I knew then and there just by looking at Leon's face that Noel wasn't coming for Christmas. "Your mother," Leon kept pronouncing angrily, "will be extremely disappointed. I hope you clearly understand, Noel, that she goes to a great deal of trouble to make Christmas here for us all and it was quite bad enough Alexandra not wanting to come because of her supposed work, but at least she had the decency to let us know several weeks ago and I can't begin to describe to you how disappointed your mother will be!"

When Leon put the receiver down, he lay on his back, not looking at me but up at the ceiling and said nothing. After a while I said: "It's not as if I *have* been to a great deal of trouble this year, Leon. I only bought the teasels because the barrow boy was so wet and I've done nothing about ordering a turkey and—"

"That's not the point!" snapped Leon. "Noel must learn that if he says he will do something, then he must do it. He'll never make a good lawyer unless he learns this."

I returned to the Margaret Drabble. Her heroine was giving birth to a baby in her own bed; the bed was saturated with the broken waters.

"Where is Noel?" I asked suddenly and I heard Leon sigh.

"He's with Alexandra," he said, "at the cottage."

16

DECEMBER 7

The thought that Leon may die illuminates for me how poorly I love myself. I really don't know what I shall do with this self, only let it trudge purposelessly about, legs taking it here and there – even to a new home, away from London which seems to me to be dying year by year just as Leon may be dying minute by minute – but soul in the deepest confusion, Sister, and heart with so feeble a love for the whole self that I sometimes feel, why did no one ever teach me to love myself, only taught me that I must put the whole world and everything in it, even the things I cannot see, before the self, so that all the world goes marching ahead of me and then round and round and round me and I am quite afraid of it. Last night I thought, if Leon dies, I must learn to love myself better and that perhaps what I should do is go back to India because from India seem to come compassionate and patient voices and in their quietness I might begin to learn. You see, even in the Oratory, Sister, whose echoing body gives me a little sense of wonder as I find the money for my candle, even in there, well, I say my prayer so quietly that no one hears it and my prayer is for Leon and not for me and I come out into the Brompton Road and I think, if only I didn't feel ashamed of everything I do.

At the Convent School one of the Sisters said to me: "We are none of us alone, Ruby, because Our Lord is always with us. If you feel lonely, think of Jesus reaching out to you as He reached out to the sinner, Mary of Magdalen, and touching you on the shoulder." And for a long time, until I left India, I used to imagine the Jesus of my picture-Bible with his crinkly hair and his long white robes putting out His hand and saying, "I am here. I am here." Until one day, I actually felt the weight of His hand on my shoulder and wondered for a while if I hadn't been Chosen. But what I never learned, Sister, was how to be quite alone without Jesus's hand on my shoulder and His picture-Bible eyes comforting me in their expressionless purity and now

17

Jesus is long since gone, unless He does come once in a while to the bathroom.

Leon, now, has never been troubled by lack of self-love and I sometimes wonder whether the whole question of loving oneself may not have a lot to do with the way, when we were children and tried to speak out for the touch and caring of our mothers or of those, such as you, Sister, whom we chose to love, the grown-ups in our world gave us their affection. And if I think for a moment of Leon's mother and of mine, I can so clearly see that – in spite of her miserliness and her whining that God had treated her unkindly by giving her such a colossal bottom that she always felt squashed to bits in a rush-hour bus and by making her family poor – Leon's mother gave him such a grandiose love that in comparison to it my mother's love for me was a little stick of a thing, gone in a minute like barley sugar and leaving no taste at all. It was as if my mother was dry of love, simply found none in her to give. And when she saw that all my life I was going to be fat like my father whom she teased and yet never laughed with and not a bit like her with her pale skin and freckles and narrow waist, she turned away from me with a sigh. Again and again I would tell her things and instead of listening, she'd just turn away. And I would wait for the sigh, almost inaudible but always there, the sighing of her weariness of India and her emptiness of love.

There isn't much time perhaps. When I went to see Leon yesterday afternoon, his right eye was open and I brought my chair very near to the bed and put my face close to his, but he didn't turn his head to look at me. I said his name quite a few times and once before when I did this he rolled his head on the pillow and stared at me. But yesterday I might just as well have said Henry Cooper or Lord Olivier, he could have been either of these and not known it just as he seemed not to know that he is Leon Constad and will die in spite of all the expensive care he's getting unless he begins to fight. I think when I go to see him this evening I shall make a fist like a Black Power athlete and grit my teeth as I do it to help him get the idea of fighting. But if he won't do this and plans to die, then Lord knows how I shall begin on all my days waiting for me, so that I can only hope and hope and even turn Catholic again in my hoping that "he will almost certainly pull through, Mrs Constad, because worse stroke cases than his have rallied – at his age – but of course it really is too early to tell . . ."

Christmas is almost here again. The barrow boys with their dyed greenery are cold and wet; Harrods is lit up. I feel sorry for the men painting the window-sills, swaying on hanging trolleys outside the flat in their white coveralls and so cold out there that now and then I ask them in and make cups of tea for them and we always talk about the weather and this day being more raw than that and will it snow for Christmas but I shouldn't think so because it's years since it did that. And I remember the way we sat, Leon and I, last Christmas Day and ate our Christmas lunch quite devoid of laughter or even kindnesses to each other, sat and were lonely and drank a bottle of claret and slept all afternoon, he on the sofa and I in our bed with the electric blanket turned on. Nobody telephoned us and we can never telephone Alexandra because there is no telephone in the cottage. In the evening, a client of Leon's, one of his co-respondents staying at the Ritz for Christmas with his girl-friend, came for a drink, though why he wanted to when he might have drunk more graciously at the Ritz Bar I really couldn't see. And Leon had also asked the Hazlehursts, who seem to spend their lives going out for drinks, and the Hazlehursts brought Gerald Tibbs, thinking he might like to get out on Christmas Day.

You could tell as soon as Gerald Tibbs walked in that he was lonely. His wife hadn't come back, hadn't even come to take her furs or the gilt-framed pictures of the children, so he said, and not a word had he had from her so that it had crossed his mind she might have been blown up on one of the chemical factory explosions you hear about in Milan. And after he'd said this, he began to drink and drink, obliterating the idea of his wife's body being blown to pieces in Italy and his hands stopped shaking and turned themselves into gesturing hands so that with his pale face he looked like a bad mime artist. Then he suddenly walked out of the room and I could hear him being sick in the lavatory, where he stayed, lying down on the floor, until I could persuade the Hazlehursts to stop drinking and take him home. Flecks of his vomit were everywhere in the lavatory, as if in his gut a bomb had exploded.

The co-respondent and his girl stayed on. The co-respondent talked to Leon about the case and the girl-friend who had left her two daughters for the bed of this man said almost nothing, as if she was killing time until she got back to the Ritz. Then, as they were leaving, she turned to me and said: "It's awfully strange, don't you think – Christmas without children?"

Leon, who had been full of professional noise while all the drink was being drunk, returned to silence as soon as the door had closed on the guests. I cleared away the glasses and the dirty ashtrays and Leon sat motionless on the sofa with one of his small cigars.

"Thank God the day's nearly over!" he said, and about ten minutes later he said this again with such loathing for all that he could see and feel and hear that I thought, oh Lord why aren't I somewhere else, why aren't I in the sunshine in the Bahamas where I've never been, only read about, sitting by a pool with my dark glasses on and an iced cocktail stuck with bits of fruit waiting for me on a cane table? Quite alone, I would go in and out of the pool all day, exercising my body and then resting it. I would talk to no one, only nod to the waiters. I would listen to some singing. Natives on a beach singing or chanting. I would watch the sun glint and glare on the water and then flame red-gold, still warm but casting long shadows, shadows of palm and beach house and of the natives still there singing on the beach, some with their brown legs calf-deep in the gentle lapping water. I would absorb all this into me, sight and sound, and then make my way to a cool room with louvered shutters, lie down on a bed and feel the burning of my skin against the cool sheets. I would lie very still on the bed, quite undisturbed and at peace.

This reminds me that when Leon was strong and full of fight and knew he wasn't Henry Cooper or Lord Olivier I now and then wanted to be rid of him, finding his miseries oppressive. That Christmas – last Christmas – he chose to be in mourning for Noel and his mourning was a dreadful thing to be with because it was so black and deep. I almost wished Leon's mother could have returned from her wide grave to make messy kosher meals for her boy and to raise her eyes to heaven now and then and say: "Sons, oh my Lord!" which was a thing she often said to me when Leon was disagreeable and I would agree, thinking of Noel with his noise and boasting. She might have made us both laugh and forget that our children had chosen not to be with us. But as it was, Leon's misery began a slow seepage into me so that I thought more and more of being in the Bahamas and away from London and from Leon, even envying Alexandra her cottage with the comforting chicken noises and its log fire, thinking anything would be better than this when Leon is never comforted by me, however hard I try.

What I didn't know was that during that Christmas it began. The shape of my family changed. And ever since, voices, some in my head such as my mother's genteel voice, and some simply whispering in my ear have said to me: "Of course, Ruby, you never should have let this happen!" And if I reply – which I seldom do, thinking to myself, why should these bossy, busy people concern themselves with my family which is so acutely a part of me and so little a part of them – I say: " 'Let' is idiocy, 'let' is irrelevant. I wasn't there."

I was in London with Leon's mood fouling my air. By the end of Boxing Day, I could *hear* the singing of the natives on the

21

beach and see the sunshine on their bodies and on mine, so much did I want to be away. I think I even talked to Leon of going to the Bahamas but he didn't listen and the day after Boxing Day when he should have gone back to the office, he didn't go and instead stayed in bed the whole day, not sleeping though he said he felt tired, but going through all the photograph albums, huge leather albums filled with his own snaps of the children, their whole lives caught there, faces changing and growing, pictured numberless times.

Leon is very fond of the albums. When he started to become rich from the river of the famous and adulterous that began to flow through his office, he bought himself a very expensive camera and with this camera at his sharp brown eye tried as hard as he could to become Cartier-Bresson. But Leon is a very bossy photographer, always telling you where to frame yourself and how to have your hands, whereas Cartier-Bresson doesn't seem to be bossy at all, so that his subjects turn out just the way they are in their panic or their joy. And it's quite difficult to believe that Cartier-Bresson didn't build himself deerstalkers' hides all over Paris, because no one in his pictures ever seems to know he's there, "and this is the way you should be, Leon," I often said, "if you want us all to be the way we are, you have to become invisible."

Another disappointing thing about Leon's photographs is that they all tend to be of people eating, because a lot of the time he forgets about trying to be Cartier-Bresson and only remembers it on picnics or on holidays in France so that hundreds of the pictures are framed by café awnings saying things like *Au Cheval Blanc* or *Chez Jacques* or by glades where the family has spread its ancient groundsheet to tuck into cold chicken and salami sandwiches. And really, going through the albums, you can imagine that all the Constad family ever does is eat or learn to ride tricycles and occasionally walk up mountains in Wales wearing anoraks, and you certainly wouldn't believe that any of us lived in London, for there's hardly a snap of it or that Noel had ever had acne because Leon never photographs anything ugly like blocks of flats or spots.

By the end of Leon's day in bed with the photograph albums he had cheered up. He smiled at me when I went in with his cold supper on a tray and the albums were in a neat pile on the floor.

"I've been through them all, Ruby," he announced, "and there are quite a few Christmases we all spent together. I dare say next year they'll both decide to come to us, especially if the cottage is cold."

"They've got a fire, Leon," I said.

"Well a fire, yes. All those old cottages have open fires, but what about the bedrooms? Ice on the window panes, I wouldn't wonder."

"I've often tried to imagine the cottage," I admitted, "I'd like to go there one day."

"I wouldn't bother, Ruby. Norfolk's a long way."

"I'd still like to go. I'd like to meet Sue and the chickens."

Leon laughed. "What the devil Noel wants to be there for I shall never know!" he said.

The following day, with Christmas well and truly over and not to be thought about any more, Leon put on his suit and went back to his office. The flat became very quiet. I cleared away all the signs of Christmas, even the teasels. Towards the end of the morning I telephoned Gerald Tibbs but no one answered. I hoovered the flat and dusted it and then got into bed with the electric blanket on and thought to myself, I can't remember how long it is since Leon and I made love; it must be months and months and no wonder if each of us feels so sad now and then because we've lost each other. We're fifty and afraid and Lord alone knows what happens to us now.

DECEMBER 8

There was a wedding at the Oratory today, Sister. I thought
they wouldn't let me in to light my candle for Leon, but they
did. I crept to the candles because all the wedding guests were
kneeling and silent as I walked in. I waited for them to start
rustling with a prayer. Over their heads, I could see the bride in
all her white net, kneeling beside her new husband who seemed
to be dressed up like a soldier, just as in India all the young men
I ever met when I left the Convent School were soldiers in my
father's regiment and thought themselves born to rule. They
kissed like rulers. They even played tennis like rulers and were
never gentle or silent in anything they did and no wonder India
heaved such a sigh and wanted to be rid of them for ever and
always. And I thought in the Oratory, poor Catholic bride with
your guardsman; better to be like you, Sister Benedicta, with a
gold ring on your left hand, bride of Christ who never touched
you, chaste all your life, than lie in a soldier's bed and hear his
shouting. I crept out of the Oratory and walked past all the
limousines waiting to take the bride and her soldier and all their
soldier friends and mothers of soldiers to a big hotel for champagne and speeches and then I began, quite unaccountably, to
weep, so that as I passed down Knightsbridge people stared at
the tears making lines through the make-up that I still put on
and I knew that on this occasion I wasn't weeping for Leon but
for my daughter and all that has happened to her since the day
Gerald Tibbs was sick on to the wall and I waited for Christmas
to end.

I should have gone from the Oratory to the nursing home to
see Leon and make my Black Power salute to rally him, but I
didn't go. It is now several days since he wrote "the aforementioned Richard Mayhew Wainwright" and each day since then
he has looked less and less capable of writing words like
"aforementioned" and it's hard to believe there's any stirring of
thought in his mind at all, so absolutely uncomprehending does

his eye look. So today I thought, let the nurses run in and out and he won't notice if I'm not there, and if he should die, then the telephone will ring and he can die while I'm there or while I'm walking down Knightsbridge, it makes no difference.

When I got home, I stopped crying. I made a cup of tea and started to imagine that I was on a train going to Norfolk, with East London and Essex and Suffolk passing by me, very cold outside the hot train, but not as cold as Norfolk where I noticed snow on the fields, getting thicker as more and more of Norfolk spread itself around me under its enormous dome of sky, then wondering where I was, whether I should get off at Norwich or go further and how in the world in all the snow would I find the little village where Alexandra lived? I imagined getting off the train not at Norwich but at a tiny station with no one there and walking off down a winding lane towards a village or small town whose church I could see in the distance. On the way I passed an old man. He was blind and carried a white stick that looked yellow against the whiter snow, but heard me pass him and mumbled: "That's not far, the pub." So I stopped and began to say to him: "Where is Alexandra? Please tell me where her cottage is. She says it's called Valley Cottage, but where is it?" But he chuckled and went on his way, saying once more: "That's not far, the pub." And soon after that the snow began to fall again, obliterating the church I had seen and I knew that I was quite lost and never should have begun.

I returned to my cup of tea in the kitchen and wondered whether it had taken Noel a long time to find the cottage the day he went there from Cambridge. It must have been quite dark by the time he got there for we were almost at the shortest day of the year with nightfall robbing all the afternoons. Perhaps he arrived at a station like the one I imagined but found there a waiting taxi to take him to Alexandra's door. Like Leon, Noel never seems to get lost, never loses direction. He would have been there by tea-time. Alexandra would have laughed to see him, wondered what on earth, Noel, when I never see you, year

25

in year out since we were little children and went to day schools? But Sue always lit the fire early on cold winter days. Noel would have smelt the fire and let the cottage take him in.

Alexandra told me that Noel stayed up all that first night talking to her about Christine. He borrowed Alexandra's mini to drive to the village and telephoned Leon. He bought two bottles of wine and a bottle of whisky at the village pub and took these back to the cottage where Sue was making a late supper. They ate the supper on the floor in front of the fire. He told Alexandra and Sue that he had stayed in bed all morning in his room in Cambridge, dreading the weeks he would have to spend with Leon and me in London. Mrs Walton had come and gone with cups of tea and little pieces of advice like other people's leavings and still Noel lay in bed, not moving until he had thought of somewhere else to go. Then he had upped and gone, taking all his things in two suitcases, everything he could cram in except his law books which he left behind in the same spirit that he was leaving Cambridge, in disgust.

I had once met Christine. Christine had been Noel's girl since their first term at Cambridge. But on the day that Leon and I met her, she chose to say almost nothing at all, just like the co-respondent's girl spending Christmas at the Ritz, except that the co-respondent's girl had been rich all her life and had jewelry and scarves to prove this in case anyone should doubt it, whereas Christine was poor and came from Liverpool and wore a coat that came from the army surplus, a long man's coat of the kind the troops wore on the Somme, only blue. Over this coat fell Christine's hair and even if, like Leon, you couldn't bear anyone who came from Liverpool because you had been born there yourself and wanted to forget it, you still had to marvel at Christine's hair which was so blond and thick it was hard to imagine it beginning at her scalp because scalps so seldom produce such a weight of beauty.

"She's not nearly good enough for Noel!" Leon thundered as we drove home from Cambridge, and I said: "It's very hard

26

to tell whether she's good enough, Leon, or not because she hardly said anything to us." But Leon had decided that he didn't approve of Christine and woe betide Noel if he should come to us and say he was going to marry Christine, woe betide him because a wife like that can get in the way of a young man's career and Noel's career was going to be brilliant, Leon was positive of that. And all this only goes to show, Sister, that there's very little compassion in Leon and there always has been very little and if you were here and could see for yourself that he is incapable of love for people with Liverpool accents, you might feel that he's unworthy of your prayers and refuse to kneel down with me in the bathroom.

Noel once believed that he loved Christine. He began to share his bed and his life with her at Cambridge and Mrs Walton, who liked Christine because she was quiet ("not like that young lady of Trevor's with her rages!") didn't mind the bed-sharing and only charged Noel 20p a day extra for Christine's breakfast. For four terms Christine's miraculous hair slept on Noel's shoulder and not until mid-way through the fourth term did we meet Christine. I dare say our meeting with Christine had something to do with what happened because on the last day of the autumn term, the day before Noel was meant to come to London, Christine left him without any warning at all and went to live with someone else. I have often thought that far from being not good enough for Noel, Christine, who was reading history and wanted to be a teacher, was probably too clever for him and in her silence the day we met her a wise person would have detected horror and disgust, not stupidity, and after that she wanted to be rid of Noel, thinking, one day he'll be like his father in a fat office and despising everyone he meets or even like his mother who long ago should have died of incomprehension and been buried with Neanderthal Man.

I couldn't blame Christine if she simply wearied of all the noise Noel made and chose quite on the spur of the moment not to listen to it any more. But Noel couldn't understand this. He couldn't believe that Christine would ever leave him for someone else until she did. And after she'd gone, he howled with all his hurt pride and swore that he'd never go back to Cambridge, swore all of this to Alexandra the night he arrived at her cottage, that he hated Cambridge, hated the street where he'd shared his room with Christine, hated the law and never wanted to see another law book as long as he lived. He spent all night swearing out his anger and drinking the whisky he'd bought at the pub until, although it was still dark, Alexandra could feel that it was near dawn and made Noel lie down in front of the fire in his sleeping-bag and crept to her own bed, angry now that he'd come to disturb the Christmas she had planned with Sue, to disrupt her routine of work and change the ways of the cottage. She lay awake in her cold bed and then went along the corridor to Sue's room and woke her up. Sue held her gently until she was warm and they went to sleep in each other's arms.

I remember imagining, Sister, when I was thirteen that one night you wouldn't send me away when sundown came. The little sisterly kisses you gave me on the top of my head, I thought the day might come when you would kiss my mouth that had never been touched except in my imagining and I would hold you and press you against me. But you never came near me, only to put your insubstantial kiss on my hair like a blessing and I wonder now if in all your life you let your body be touched or if you hid it there under the grey and white robe, bride of Christ, until it was old and wrinkled and they buried it unloved. Poor Sister Benedicta, where on earth did you go when all the soldiers were marched out of India and the Convent School was closed and the daughters of the high-ranking officers sent packing? Did you mourn the daughters of the high-ranking officers? Did you for ever remember the day of the grand "welcome" pageant for the Viceroy with all your favourite girls arching and bending and stretching for the Viceroy under the rows of bunting pinned up by the nuns in the big ugly hall? Did you think, forever, oh that was the day! the day the Viceroy and the Vicereine came to the Convent School and the school band played as proudly as any corps of Royal Marines? I wonder if you came to England and where you hid them, all your memories of India?

It is late at night now and I have begun to feel very guilty that I didn't go to see Leon today. Since he went into the nursing home, I have been every day – usually in the afternoons, as instructed by Matron – until today. It occurs to me that though he can't tell me this, Leon may look forward to my visits. For what does his day consist of, or his night for that matter, the two being indistinguishable for the blind in his room is always down and a light on, except that at night he may hear the nursing home quieten down and see his flowers being taken out and watch his night nurse dozing in her chair, bringing herself to orgasm, thinking he doesn't know what my hands are doing, doesn't hear my little sighs and shudders. But if he sees the night nurse, if he can write "night nurse" and know what he means, then surely he sees me and knows who I am? But he never gives me the least sign of recognition and sitting there watching him, I wonder if he's thinking who on earth is this fat woman coming day after day and staring at me and really I'd be much happier if she never came back again, for what is she but another confusion in the sea of all my confusions?

So perhaps after all it doesn't matter if I go to see Leon or not. But I can never be quite certain of this, never know for sure that he doesn't wait for me and it would be dreadful to think of him lying there and waiting and then seeing his flowers being taken out and know that it was night-time and that I never came when the night nurse was there in her chair and the nursing home was quiet. He wouldn't know that I hadn't decided never to go there again. He wouldn't know that only yesterday I planned to arrive full of vigour in his room and do the Black Power salute I've been practising in front of the mirror to help him get the idea of fighting and never giving up until he has pieced himself back together again and triumphed absolutely over any idea that might be lurking in his mind about being Lord Olivier or Richard Mayhew Wainwright, whoever he may be. He might try to ask the night nurse where I was by reaching for the slate which I have told them they must always leave handy, day or night, and writing something on it like "fat, grey-haired woman" or "lady with crocodile handbag", having come to the conclusion somewhere inside himself that my presence in his room nudges him into sensible thoughts about himself and better I was there – even if it takes him months to remember who I am – than not there, because no one else ever goes to see him, knowing how ill he is, thinking that's a waste of time going to see Leon Constad when he can't say a single word or even sit up and look at his flowers.

I have read out all the cards to him, the little florist's cards that arrived with the pots of chrysanthemums and bunches of hothouse daffodils and freesias and irises his clients have sent. They mostly say rather formal things like "sincere good wishes for your recovery" or "sincere good wishes for your speedy recovery", but one of them said "bon voyage" which seems so unnecessarily pessimistic and cruel that I feel it must be a florist's error and that those flowers should be sitting in someone's cabin on an ocean liner bound for Hawaii or even for the Bahamas where last year I so longed to be. Perhaps, if Leon discovers who he is again, I could take him there and in the sunshine he would learn to run again and swim and I would watch him running on the beach and think, thank God he didn't die. Although I am probably quite mistaken in thinking we might find peace in the Bahamas or even hear the singing that I once imagined. Because the Bahamas is undoubtedly one of those places where countless white Englishwomen and American women believe they'll find peace and hear natives singing and in consequence there is no peace at all because the white people make so much noise snapping their fingers for waiters and bellyflopping into swimming pools that you can't hear yourself think and you never hear the natives singing because

30

the natives are utterly miserable most of the time, cutting cane
for a pittance, and don't feel like singing.

We'll go somewhere else, Leon. We might go to a Swiss
mountain-top in the spring and do breathing exercises and see
the wild narcissi come out.

DECEMBER 9

I dreamt about Noel last night. In all my dreams about Noel I am always angry with him. I cry with anger. Sometimes I wish I knew where he was so that I could talk to him and let my anger burst out and didn't have to keep dreaming it and dreaming it.

In this dream, Noel was dressed up like a soldier without a single crease in his smart, stretched uniform. He was playing tennis and laughing. He won every point and each time he laughed and then I saw that his opponent was an old, old Indian woman in a sari and shawl who was holding the racket all wrongly and couldn't run at all because she was too weak and infirm. "Stop that, Noel!" I shouted, "Stop playing and making the old woman run!" But he only laughed and kept announcing the score in the clipped voice of a Wimbledon umpire: "Thir-tay love! For-tay love! Game to Constad!"

Waking from this dream, I thought of a thing you used to say at the convent school, Sister. "Anger is not wrong, Ruby," you said. "When Jesus went into the temple and saw the money-lenders and the traders occupying God's holy place, He was angry. He shouted! Only remember, Ruby, that each time you feel anger, you must ask yourself why. You must know why." And so I lay very still and tried to understand why, not very far inside me, crouches a huge store of anger for Noel. And I know that I blame Noel for everything that has happened. I say to myself, "It couldn't possibly be my fault: I was at home, I did nothing. I wandered up and down Knightsbridge in the rain and waited for Christmas. It's not my fault that Leon's dying in a private room, it's Noel's fault." But really I can't be certain either of Noel's guilt or of my innocence. I'm like the doctors – I don't know. I only want to believe that I had nothing to do with it.

I telephoned Mrs Walton. I thought, perhaps after all Noel is back in Cambridge, even though term is almost over. I wanted to say to Noel: "I've been blaming you and blaming you, but who's to say for certain if you are to blame? Who's to say that Leon's stroke wasn't written on his palm when he struggled free of Grandma Constad's enormous womb? And perhaps after all, Noel, we could meet, even for half an hour, and I would try to rid myself of this anger and then we could start again trying to find some love for each other, mother and son."

"Noel?" Mrs Walton said, "Oh no, dear, Noel won't be coming back."

"How do you know, Mrs Walton? Has he told you definitely?"

"Oh definitely, dear, yes."

"Did he write to you? Because the last time I telephoned you, you hadn't heard from him and you didn't know . . ."

"Well, I had a card, yes."

"A card?"

"Yes. He asked me to give his books to Trevor."

"Did he?"

"Yes. A card from France, you see."

"Yes, I see."

"Now Trevor's here. Would you like a word with Trevor?"

"No. It was only Noel I wanted – on the off chance . . ."

Noel is afraid. If he knew his father was dying and couldn't say a word, he might come home. As it is, he may stay in France for ever, though how he's living and where I can't imagine, because living anywhere at all in France seems to cost such a lot that it makes you wonder whether everybody there, even the boys on mopeds and the cashiers at the Credit Lyonnais, isn't a millionaire, for how else could they go on spending so much and getting so little and never being heard to say: "*Ah non, alors!*"

Noel was always frightened of Leon's Jewish anger. Jewish anger seems to burst out of Jewish people in a particular kind of way, with an astonishing fluency, words gushing and tumbling as if a hose had been turned on inside them by their two-

33

thousand-year-old memory of pogroms and atrocities and there is no stopping them. Grandma Constad's two-thousand-year-old memory of pogroms always seemed to be at its most alert on London buses in the rush hour when she felt her huge bum being pressed against some tired typist and as she grew older and wider her angry monologues got longer and longer until one day an extremely sensible West Indian bus conductor said to her: "You shut up your complainin', mam, or I put you off at di next stop and never mind Moses!" And I don't know if, after that, Grandma Constad ever went on another London bus because the West Indian conductor frightened her into silence, and as Grandma Constad was so seldom silent, I can only think that she must have suddenly remembered all the black people in the world who work down mines and live their lives in anger and grief and have to tell their children that life is anger and life is grief and that she felt ashamed.

I dare say Noel feels ashamed of what he did. I feel ashamed of it, Sister Benedicta, because all that Alexandra has said seems to tell me that it was done quite without love.

It had to do with Christine, undoubtedly. When Noel got to Alexandra's cottage, all he wanted to do was talk about Christine. He let his hurt pride talk: he drank and swore and thought the drinking and swearing would heal his wound. But the next day, when he woke up in his sleeping-bag by the embers of the fire, fogged from the whisky and cold, he discovered that his wound was still there and he wanted to cry. Sue and Alexandra were up and had had breakfast. Sue was working in the garden and Alexandra was in the garage where she'd made herself a studio. They had seen Noel huddled asleep in his bag and had left him to sleep on, and once they had each begun their work they forgot about him until he woke up and began shouting for Alexandra. She heard him shouting and came in and saw that he looked quite lost and abject and thought, I can't send him away – as she had planned with Sue in the early morning – and instead made him sit down in the kitchen while she cooked eggs for him

34

and then stayed and talked to him, thinking after all he's my brother whom I hardly know, not since we were kids and went to Miss Forester's school.

Sue came in with muddy hands and four eggs she'd collected from the coop. Less than six eggs from her hens and Sue was disappointed and when she saw that Alexandra had stopped work to make breakfast for Noel she felt cross, knowing that Alexandra had decided to let him stay. She sulked out in the garden for the rest of the day. Alexandra went out to her and said: "Sue, I'm sorry. Please understand that I can't send Noel away and let's try and make the best of it." But Sue couldn't see that there was any "best" to be made. She went on with her digging and said nothing, so Alexandra wandered away and tried to get on with her painting, only she found she couldn't work because she felt trapped.

She thought about herself and Sue. She asked herself if she loved Sue and knew that she didn't. Yet she had been very content to let Sue love her, finding in Sue's passion for her a kind of exhilaration she had never felt with a man. Sue would love women all her life; she would never love a man, couldn't bear the hardness or the smell of a man's body, but often wept with joy when she felt another woman's shape and softness under her. She knew she was good at loving them. Her fingers and tongue could make them shout with pleasure. "I'm good," she announced to Alexandra the first time she had taken her to bed, and Alexandra, who had never imagined until that night that she would make love with a woman had been shy and awkward, thinking as she lay there, what am I doing and what turn is my life taking? Then, to her surprise, she found she felt no guilt. Rather, she began to feel very content with Sue's love and with her life which, for the first time, seemed free from confusion. There was the cottage and there was her work at the Art School and there was Sue. She gave to nothing and no one else any time or attention, scarcely a thought even, so that Leon and I were among those she had come to forget and all of these

35

forgettings mattered very little to her because she had found some peace.

When Alexandra described to me what her life at the cottage had been like before Noel arrived, this was the word she used: peace. And I thought of the fathomless complexity of that word, knowing that I have hardly dared to use it since I was a girl and thought I had found it, Sister, sitting in your room with the sunset coming on. And yet I know that there was no peace in India and the sun glaring through your raffia blinds set on a false peace that the British wives of soldiers and sons and daughters of soldiers chose to believe in, safe inside their big houses behind tall white walls. And even you believed it, didn't you Sister? thinking in your little nun's heart, I shall be here for ever in the Convent School with the daughters of the high-ranking officers, and India – the India of the poor tin houses and the bazaars – will never creep in, I will never come face to face with India as long as I live.

When Alexandra described the peace she thought she had found, I didn't say: "There is no peace anywhere, unless perhaps it is the peace of God that passeth all understanding and certainly passeth mine and always has done", but I listened and listened and tried to come close to imagining her life with Sue in the cottage that I've never seen. Alexandra knew and Sue knew that the peace had gone the night Noel walked in. It was as if a soldier had come to arrest them.

I went to see Leon this afternoon. He showed no sign of having noticed my absence yesterday. One of the nurses looked at me accusingly, but I've often noticed that nurses have a way of looking at people accusingly, even at patients lying there with their legs on pulleys or their stomachs stitched up from top to bottom, and so I won't infer anything from the look this nurse gave me and on the contrary feel rather cheered that Leon picked up his slate today and wrote "How long". I couldn't answer this of course, not knowing for certain whether it was a question or a comment and, if a question, to what it referred. "How long have I been here?" "How long shall I have to stay?" "How long will it be before I can get up?" "How long will it be before I know who I am and who you are and what has happened?" It could be any of these. I just don't know. So I took the slate and rubbed out Leon's "How long" and wrote "I don't know" and showed this to him, hoping it might prompt him to ask a more explicit question in order to get a more satisfactory answer. But he stared at the slate quite blankly for a few seconds and then closed his eyes and never opened them again, even when it was time for me to go.

I tried talking to him as I often do. But today I didn't talk about the difficulty of getting taxis or the price of flowers; I asked him if he remembered things. I asked him if he remembered being a law student in London and meeting me for the first time. "Do you remember, Leon," I said, "how we met in the house of Max Reiter, the Austrian Jewish composer who had married my godmother Louise and teased her out of her Catholic ways until she wrapped up all her pictures of the Holy Family in calico and packed them away with mothballs? Do you remember Max Reiter? You came to dinner and I was there. You came with another Jewish boy, a student of Max's. The Reiters always liked everyone to bring their friends, and chairs and place mats and extra portions of food appeared as if by magic for all these friends and no one ever complained, not even the cook. Do your remember Godmother Louise? She was in love with Max Reiter all her life. They used to make love very often, even when they were old, she told me. And yet they never had any children. They hadn't got the time really because Max Reiter was always off on tours to Paris and Salzburg and Vienna and Rome and Godmother Louise always went with him so that they could make love in hotel bedrooms and never be separate from each other.

"My mother always used to say Godmother Louise was barren. My mother said God had punished Louise with barren-

37

ness because she'd wrapped her pictures of the Virgin Mary in calico and stuffed them away. My mother didn't like me going to see Louise after she wasn't a Catholic any more; she tried to divest Louise of her godmothership! But I used to love the Reiters' house in St John's Wood that was always full of friends and friends of friends and where you never saw a soldier and no one talked about tea parties or tennis. I used to ask myself there as often as I could and I never believed in Louise's barrenness – even though I was still a Catholic then and went to Mass every Sunday – because Max Reiter once said: 'We don't need children of our own, do we Louise, when we have Ruby and we have all my students?' And Louise laughed and looked happy and in the Bible barren people never seem happy or full of laughter, but walk around with shawls over their heads, getting older and older and more and more barren and you know there's no hope for them unless God does a miracle. And I know that Louise wasn't barren and could have conceived hundreds of children in hotel rooms alone, but that all she wanted in her life was to be with Max and this was enough."

I stopped at this point, crept to the bed and looked very closely at Leon. He seemed to be asleep, breathing quite easily and I thought of leaving. I wondered if the effort of writing "How long" on the slate had exhausted him. Then it occurred to me that if he was resting as peacefully as he seemed to be, perhaps my talking soothed him and stopped him feeling afraid. For I have a suspicion – from the way his right eye looks when it's open – that he is afraid. Perhaps his own silence terrifies him. Once or twice one side of his mouth has moved a little, as if he was trying to speak.

I sat down again and whispered my little reminiscences to Leon and to the flowers, thinking neither Leon nor the flowers hears them. Twice a nurse came in to look at Leon and on the second occasion stood at his bedside and took a pulse reading. I didn't stop talking. I reminded Leon that he had been a very shy person when I met him that evening at Max Reiter's house, "not like the person you became, Leon," I said, "so full of fight and proud of your big office and all your telephones. You had all the words and fight inside you, I expect, but you just weren't using them very much then, not that evening anyway, but you chose to talk rather quietly to me. You told me you were working so hard to pass your law exams that you never had time to go to dinners and meet people and that you were only there because your friend Philip had insisted and because you had once heard a snatch of Max Reiter's music on the Third Programme.

"I told you that Louise was my godmother, that I came to the house often when Max and Louise weren't abroad, and I believe, Leon, that you only decided to like me because of this, because you had discovered that you enjoyed being away from your law books in the house of a composer and wanted the Reiters to ask you there again. I say this, you see, because what else was there in me to like? I wasn't fat then at twenty-two, but still plump. I couldn't talk about law or music – the things that interested you. All I knew was India. Louise and Max pitied me for being a child of the Empire and wanted to teach me how to forget it. 'India!' Louise used to say, 'I marvel that anyone ever thought that could last!' So I wonder what we talked about sitting there at the dinner table at the first of all our meetings. I can't remember."

I left the nursing home soon after that, not wanting to go on because of the nurses coming in and out and listening to everything I said. On my way out, I stood at the door for a moment, remembering my Black Power salute, but I didn't do it. There didn't seem any point when Leon's eyes were closed and he couldn't see it.

I asked the taxi that picked me up in Harley Street to take me to the Oratory. After the glare of Leon's little room I thought I would try to find you, Sister Benedicta, in that vaulted darkness and ask you to help me pray. I knelt down and tried to think of a prayer but not a word would come to me today, not a word, no God, not even the ghost of a nun, five foot two with her arms folded. I got up and went to light my candle, stood and watched it flicker and tried to calculate how long it would burn.

DECEMBER 11

One confusion is at last resolved. I know now who "the aforementioned Richard Mayhew Wainwright" is. Today there was a ring on my doorbell (strange occurrence these days because nobody calls, knowing that if they did call, they wouldn't know what to say to me) and when I opened the door, there on the mat stood a lean woman with faded hair calling herself Evelyn Wainwright, holding her handbag to her as if it was a china plate and might break, and asking to see Leon. I was so surprised that anyone should ask for Leon that an immediate and totally unexpected statement burst out of me. "Leon's dead!" I said, and seeing Evelyn Wainwright's look of disbelief, had to qualify this by stammering: "Well, when I say he's dead, I mean he's not absolutely dead. He could die any day."

It seemed only fair, after this dreadful confusion to ask the woman in. We went into the drawing-room and she sat down on the edge of the sofa, still clutching her handbag and I waited for her to explain why she had called. She stared at me, sizing me up. Then she looked round the room.

"It's not as grand as his office, is it?" she said.

"Leon's office?"

"Mr Constad's, yes."

"Do you know," I said, "I don't remember the office very well. He had so many. He started with a very small one in an alleyway off Fleet Street. It was over a gymnasium and you could hear people thumping about all the time."

After a pause, Evelyn Wainwright said: "He *is* ill then?"

"Yes, he's very ill. He had a stroke."

"I shouldn't have come then. You see, I didn't believe them at Mr Constad's office – that secretary of his – I didn't believe he wasn't there. I thought the secretary was hiding him and not letting me see him. I mean, they do this, the secretaries of important men: they hide them."

Evelyn Wainwright was moving nearer and nearer to the

41

edge of the sofa and nearer to the edge of tears. I thought she might bump down on to her thin bottom with a wail.

"Would you like a cup of tea?" I asked.

"Yes," she said. And the word sounded like a click coming from the back of her throat. I got up. It's a long time since I've made a cup of tea for anyone but the window-sill painters.

"Please do relax, Mrs Wainwright," I said feebly and went to the kitchen. While I was there making the tea, I longed to peep back into the drawing-room and see if Evelyn Wainwright had let herself tumble back into the sofa. I realized that I wanted to keep the woman there until I had quite unravelled the mystery of her and discovered her connection with "the aforementioned Richard Mayhew Wainwright", imagining that all of this was very important and would reveal to me more about the true state of Leon's mind than anything the doctors had told me.

When I went in with the tea, Evelyn Wainwright was standing at the french windows looking down on to the street, in the way that Leon had stood watching for Noel on the day that Noel never arrived.

"Tea!" I said, and she turned round with a look of surprise. Then she crossed to the sofa and perched on it again, but this time without her handbag which had fallen to the floor.

"I won't stay long," she said.

"Oh," I said, pouring the tea, "you can stay as long as you like. I expect I shall go to see Leon this afternoon, but I've really got nothing to do until then."

"I wouldn't have thought of intruding on you – at a time like this. It was only that I didn't believe them, you see. They said: 'You can see Mr Partridge if you like,' but I knew that Mr Partridge was young – younger than my son – and he wouldn't have done a good job for me. So I said: 'No, I must see Mr Constad. Mr Constad is the best. I've been told that he's the best and I must have the best man or what hope do I have of winning my case?' You see, Mr Constad – your husband – had mentioned this Partridge before. He said he was too busy to take on my case, but this Partridge would look after me. But 'No', I said, 'I can choose who I want and I've been told you're the best and my son will pay. It's not as if you're not going to get your money.' "

I had poured Evelyn Wainwright a cup of tea and she tried to take a sip of it straightaway, but it was too hot and she went on talking. She didn't look at me as she talked, but at a fixed point straight ahead of her on the carpet, as if she was trying to balance.

"You see, I know I have a case. I know that with a clever man to speak up for me, I could win. But it's not a usual case, you see, mother against son, and I knew Mr Constad didn't want to take me on. He wanted to give me to Partridge, but I said no. And then the next time I went to see him – I had an appointment with him – his secretary said: 'Mr Constad can't see you today, but Mr Partridge will see you.' So I said: 'What is all this? It isn't as if my son won't have to pay and I want to see the best man. I need a really good man, or I shall lose. With Partridge I'll lose, I know I will.' So I went home without seeing anyone. I wouldn't see Partridge.

"Then a day or two later, I rang up for an appointment with Mr Constad and that secretary said: 'Oh no, I'm afraid Mr Constad is ill and won't be available for some time. Can I suggest you see Mr Partridge?' So I said again: 'What is all this? Maybe I'm not Burt Lancaster, but I can pay!' And all she'd say was, 'Mr Constad's been taken ill. He's very ill and can't see anyone.' "

Evelyn Wainwright's eyes blinked faster and faster as she spoke. She tried her tea again, took a sip, then another and on the third sip looked up at me.

"I'm not explaining myself well, am I?" she said, "You see, since all this has happened, my nerves have been terrible. I know what it is now to suffer from nerves and I never thought I would because I never suffer from any kind of nervous complaint and now I can't sleep or do anything properly because all I

43

can think of is my home being sold under my feet, just taken away from me and I'm quite powerless. And your husband was the one man, you see, they told me might win my case – the one man. And now of course he's ill and can't help me and I know I won't win with Partridge. Partridge is younger than my son!"

After a pause, during which Evelyn Wainwright drank the rest of the tea, I said: "I'd like to know more about it, Mrs Wainwright. Perhaps, if my husband recovers, he could do something for you . . ."

"Oh no. It's quite wrong of me to have come. I didn't know he was really ill, you see. I thought that was just a downright lie. He's in the hospital then?"

"Yes. In a nursing home. He gets very good care."

"And when will he be out, Mrs Constad? I keep asking them at his office, but they say they can't say."

"No, well, no one can say really. He's had a very severe stroke. He just lies there and we all wait and wonder."

"I'm sorry if he's ill. I dare say there must be other people, solicitors I mean, who could help me win, but I was told your husband was the very best. They said he'd fight for me."

"Well, I'm sure he would have done. Though he doesn't win all his cases. He's lost some quite important ones. I expect he would have tried to win yours. He always tries to win."

"I need a fighter, you see Mrs Constad. Someone who can stand up and say there's right on my side. Because I know there is. I mean, I've lived in my house for thirty-seven years. Thirty-seven years! And now Richard's just taking it away from me and selling it. I walk by the estate agent's window and there it is, For Sale – my house!"

"Well, if the house is yours, Mrs Wainwright . . ."

"It's *not* mine, that's just it; it's Richard's. I made it over to him years ago when my husband died so that when I die it will be his and he wouldn't have to sell it to pay the duty. But I never dreamed he'd turn me out. It's greed, that's all it is, greed and debts. He just wants the money. He doesn't care about the way

44

I feel. And there's nothing written down to say he can't sell it. That's why your husband didn't want to take me on. He said 'There's nothing written down to say he can't sell it.' "

"It does seem rather odd not to have written that down . . ." I began, but Evelyn Wainwright wouldn't let me interrupt, she just wanted to go on.

"Family solicitors, you see," she said, "when they drew up the document giving the house to Richard, they never dreamed that Richard wouldn't let me stay on. There was a Clause 3 (they never should have been allowed to write that Clause 3, your husband said) and all they put down was that Richard should make provision – 'adequate provision' they wrote – for me if for any reason the house was sold. And I remember Richard laughed and said: 'We'll never sell the old house, we're all much too fond of it and I don't think Mother could live anywhere else.' So I never dreamed, did I? And who would have dreamed that one's own son . . .? And it's only greed, that's all it is, greed and debts. And I said: 'Why don't you sell your own house, Richard? Why don't you go and live in a bungalow?' But he won't entertain the idea. 'I've got a family,' he says, 'and we need a big place, whereas you, you don't need a huge old house like that any more, do you Mother? You're lost in it.' "

"It's very large, is it Mrs Wainwright?"

"No, not at all, it's a family house – five bedrooms. And I manage perfectly well and I love every room in it. And whatever will I do in a wretched bungalow with this 'integral garage' whatever that's meant to mean? I mean, I've been to see it and if I live to be a hundred, I'll never think of it as home. I never will. But I'm powerless, you see and do you think that's right, Mrs Constad? Do you?"

I was trying hard to imagine Evelyn Wainwright's house and her in it. I saw a lot of shabby things and moulting animals on rugs and I thought, she must have been lonely and neglected a long time to be so full of rage.

45

"I don't know," I said, "I've never been very good at judging things. I often get everything quite wrong. But I dare say when it comes to court, you'll be allowed to stay on. Judges don't like young men selling things off, they have a hatred for this, in fact."

"How do you know this, I mean, when there's no clause to say he mustn't sell?"

"I used to go to court quite a lot. It used to interest me. And I got to know quite a bit about the ways of judges. There are no young judges, you see. They're all old. They make all the noises of old people, squeaks and wheezes and farts, which can be quite distracting in the middle of an important trial. They never notice their old-men's noises, but everyone else does and really it's enough to make you lose faith in them. But what I can tell you is that they hate the idea of anyone selling anything off. It's as if they saw their gowns being sold next and their wigs and their latchkeys to rooms in the Middle Temple."

Evelyn Wainwright looked at me as if I was mad. I realized that I was smiling and that my smile was inappropriate. I took it off my face (it seemed a long, long time since a smile had been there) and offered Evelyn Wainwright some more tea. She shook her head.

"No, I can't stay any longer," she said, "and I wouldn't have bothered you if I had known your husband really was ill. Perhaps when you go to see him – unless he doesn't want to be bothered with work – you could remind him about my case and tell him I'm refusing to see Partridge and then when he comes out of hospital, he might be able to give me some time. I mean, I may not be Burt Lancaster, but . . ."

I thought, if you could see Leon, Evelyn Wainwright, see him the way he is now. "Your case is on his mind," I said curtly.

"Is it? Well, if it's on his mind, he'll take me on won't he? He'll fight for me?"

"He might die."

"Oh no! He couldn't die, could he? I mean what a waste! A

man who can fight like him and people need other people to fight for them, don't they?"

"Sometimes, perhaps."

"He won't die, will he?"

"I don't know."

"Oh, he mustn't die."

"I'll show you out, shall I?"

"Yes. I looked you up in the telephone book, you see. That's how I found you. I thought, Mr Constad is so well protected he won't be in the telephone directory but there he was. I was very surprised. I didn't think, with his reputation and protection he'd be in the book."

When we were at the door, I thought suddenly, I never want to see her again and I said: "Please don't wait for Leon, will you? Please go and see Partridge. Partridge will help you."

"He won't, Mrs Constad. He won't. I need the best and I'll wait and Richard will have to pay the costs, the judge will see to that."

And then she was gone, the lift swallowing her and I thought of her driving back to her home and putting out dog food in old plastic bowls and birdseed in little trays. I don't know why I imagined her with pets; I believe she must have smelt of animal fur and faded blankets and I found her repulsive. I couldn't feel sad for her, though I tried. I sympathized with the son Richard who wanted the old home gone and his mother out of the way and safe in a centrally heated bungalow with shiny floors.

But why is her case on Leon's mind? Does Leon remember her and her rage? Or is there nothing of her at all inside him, only the disembodied phrase "the aforementioned Richard Mayhew Wainwright" which he may not even recognize as a name, just as a kind of pattern his mind keeps making? I think what I must do this afternoon is to tell him that Evelyn Wainwright has been here to see me and watch him closely for any sign that this information is helpful to him.

47

It occurs to me that he might be feeling guilty about this case, which doesn't seem to bear much resemblance to his others, which are all very brightly coloured and this is rather a faded one and for this reason wouldn't have appealed to him and he may even have sat there saying to himself, "I wish this poor washed-out woman was Burt Lancaster." Or perhaps it was this case that made him understand at last that often the law is quite rigid and arbitrary like a bad headmaster who thinks that he sets to rights everything that is wrong in the school. Perhaps he at last noticed that the law only solves half of what it thinks it solves and that in some cases it is quite fumbling and inappropriate and what is needed is something else. In his long silence, perhaps Leon is determining what the "something else" is and may reveal it one day, when he's discovered it. But I have my doubts. Leon has always had such faith in the law and all the thousand ringings of his green telephone and his red telephone and his white telephone have never made him lose that faith, and as far as anyone can tell, it must be with him still.

When Noel was born, Leon came into the ward and took the baby out of my arms, held it up and looked at it very closely and then said a strange thing. He said: "I see myself," as if the red-faced baby was a mirror and I laughed. But Leon was serious. All through Noel's life, he has wanted the boy to be like him. It was Leon's idea – and once this was in his head, it wouldn't come out of it – to call the baby Noel, his own name spelt backwards. And he kept on looking at Noel, trying to see himself take shape in him. "My son is very like me!" he so often announces to people who've never met Noel and then I always think, there he goes again with that old twaddle, because Noel isn't really at all like Leon and I don't think he ever will be. He doesn't look a bit like Leon, for a start, but resembles my mother and all her rather tall relatives who were narrow-boned, straight-haired and freckled. There's not a freckle on Leon's body. And Noel is a loud person, clumsy, too big for the room; he's inherited nothing of Leon's neatness and sharp efficiency.

48

I don't know why Leon has always wanted Noel to be like him. It sounds very like conceit, but I know it isn't this – it's far too desperate a hope. I once asked Grandma Constad if she understood why Leon clung to this hope, but all she said was: "Sons, oh my Lord, and sons of sons!" which revealed to me only that she didn't know, just as she didn't seem to know about a great many things in the world such as where the Pope lived (she though it was Dublin) and why the seats on London buses weren't wider. "I only know about being poor. That's all I know about," she once announced to me. But she said this long after she was rich and Leon had bought her a house in Chelsea, and whenever I think about her now, I have to conclude that she was rather a stupid woman and only said meaningless things like "Sons, oh my Lord!" to fill up all the blanks in her mind.

I discovered that talking to Evelyn Wainwright had made me tired. I'm not used to talking to anyone. I say my monologues in Leon's room with the nurses coming and going, but there I can stop talking whenever I like and I never have to listen to anyone else because Leon is mute. I think the listening tired me. I found that after I had wondered a little about the Wainwright case, and its place in Leon's subconscious, I felt a terrible weariness seeping into me, as if my blood was flowing so slowly it could hardly get round me, and I didn't know what to do with my body except lie it down.

One of the painters on his trolley was painting my bedroom window. He is Irish and the cheeriest of painters and I long for him to say "top o' the mornin' ", only he never does and I really can't blame him because the mornings are all cold and grey as sorrow. I waved to him and he gave me a kind of salute with his brush and then I caught a brief glimpse of his startled eye as I drew the bedroom curtains and shut him out. It was lunchtime, but I wasn't hungry and I knew that unless I could rest for a while, I wouldn't get to the nursing home in the afternoon.

49

I didn't get to the nursing home. I dreamed away the whole afternoon, not waking when it got dark, sleeping an exhausted, dream-filled sleep.

I was on my train again going towards Norfolk, but this time the snow had fallen so thickly, drifted so dangerously, that the train had to keep stopping. There were great mountains of snow on the line that had to be shovelled away before the train could go on. Men came up with shovels. The men were dressed like the navvies who broke their backs building the Stockton and Darlington in the 1820s, and I thought with all the muscle and strength in them they would clear the snow in no time and we could go on. But I leant out of my carriage window and I could see the mountain of snow and the men with shovels and I knew that they were working dreadfully slowly, taking their time, not caring whether the train moved off or whether it sat on that lonely bit of Eastern Region line until nightfall – until daybreak. I climbed out of the train and I was ankle-deep in the snow on the side of the track. I walked to where the navvies were shovelling away the snow mountain and I said: "Tell me where the blind man is with his stick. He knows where the pub is, and if I can just get to the pub, then someone there will tell me where I am." The navvies shook their heads and looked at each other and then back at me, as if they hadn't understood a word I'd said. I asked them again, pleaded with them, "tell me where the blind man is", but they stared at me now like people stare at lunatics and one of them gestured towards the great expanse of snow-covered plough that stretched away to my right towards the great weight of the sky and I looked in vain for a road, the road where I'd first met the blind man, but there was no road.

I noticed then that from all the carriage windows, people were staring at me. Along the whole length of the train they were staring and gaping, so that I became afraid of them and afraid to get back into the train and I wandered off across the white furrowed field. The furrows were as hard as granite, so that with each stride my ankles gave and my feet twisted and it was an agony to go on.

I walked until the train was almost out of sight. I looked back at it, immobile in the snowscape, and felt suddenly glad, proud of myself that I had abandoned the train and gone my own way. It was getting quite dark in a moonless afternoon, but ahead of me now I could see a light. I was glad to be following a light, thinking to myself the light is the pub and it will be warm in there and the landlord will say: "There's not a field for miles around that I don't know like the back of my hand, nor a house for that matter," and the great grey expanse of the dark Norfolk day will be tamed by this one man's knowledge of it. But then I knew that the light wasn't the pub; the light was Alexandra's cottage. I had found it quite by chance, by stumbling off the train and over the plough. I was within fifty yards of it and I thought, now at last I shall see.

When I reached the cottage, I didn't know whether to knock at the back door or the front. I waited at the back door and listened. There wasn't a sound. I knocked feebly and then noticed that the door was ajar. I crept in.

I found myself in a small kitchen. The light was on, but the room was empty. There were crayons and paints all over the kitchen table. On a very old cooker, there was a pan of boiling water with one egg in it. The bubbling egg was the only sound.

I was very cold and I wanted to find the room with the log fire. So I walked out of the kitchen into a passage. The passage was dark, but I felt my way along it to a heavy door that opened with a Suffolk latch. I could see a light behind the door and I thought, now I have found Alexandra.

I was in the room. The room was small and untidy and smelt of paint. There was a fire in it, but the fire had burned low and no warmth from it reached me because there was a girl kneeling in front of it. I knew that the girl was Sue. I said: "Sue, I've come across all the fields from the train. I dared to get off the train and follow the navvy's pointing hand, so don't tell me that

51

it was all in vain." Sue turned round and stared at me, but said nothing, only stared. So I said again: "Sue, don't tell me that Alexandra isn't here. I've come here to be with you both and I promise not to disturb the hens and all I want is to understand. Please don't tell me to go away."

Sue still said nothing, but turned back to the fire. And it was then that I remembered I had brought a paraffin heater with me on the train and had left it there when I clambered down into the snow. I understood then that Sue would only talk to me if I went back and fetched the heater. I had come empty-handed and she scorned me and would tell me nothing until I had gone back to the train and fetched my gift for the cottage. Yet at the same time, I also knew that the mountain of snow on the line had been shovelled away by now and the navvies had gone home to their tea and the train had rushed on into the darkness towards the sea and the paraffin heater was lost.

"I could go . . ." I began to say, "but how could I ever catch the train. Even if I ran and ran, I could never catch the train. . . ."

It was five o'clock and London was noisy outside the closed curtains. I went to the bathroom and said a prayer. "Oh God," I said, "I'm afraid."

The painters are finishing off today, so they told me. The window-sills are white and smooth again and the rust that bleeds from the iron balcony has been healed for a while by a coat of black paint. When I go to see Leon today, which of course I must, I may tell him that the flat is looking better now and say: "If only you could come home, Leon, and see it, before it starts flaking and decaying again. If only you could come now."

If Leon does come home one day, talking, moving, knowing who he is, I shall try to love him better, Sister. Because when I think of all my years with Leon, I know that I have been like a big snail, lumbering round the corners of his life with half myself inside me. That is how it feels, and I marvel that Leon, with his quick-talking mind and his neat legs, has been able to bear the sight of me. I have moved so slowly, got in everybody's way. I have been huge and purposeless. When I met Leon and began to love him, Godmother Louise was full of wonder: "You are transformed, Ruby! You are beautiful! Now you can understand, can't you, what it is to love?" But I don't believe I understood love, though I told Louise that of course I did and that my love for Leon would endure summer and winter as hers had done and that if ever Leon was rich, we would travel across Europe making love in hotel bedrooms and never bear to be parted. But all I understood really was a feeling of belonging. I knew that I wanted to belong, to merge, to lose myself. And Leon had such a sure sense of his own identity and was so absolutely purposeful in all that he did, that within a very short time I had put away most of myself – all the self that you knew, Sister, and had a mind to cherish in your way – and seemed to exist only through Leon.

There have been moments when Leon has wanted to be rid of me. "This snail," I expect he said to himself, "with half her being tucked away ever since I met her and the rest creeping (quite without any understanding of the world except the understanding that I give it) so painfully slowly, fatly, backwards and forwards across all my days, I must get away from this snail now, at once, before it falls on me and crushes me." And he went away, taking almost nothing but the weight of his unspent love in his balls and for a while he kept diving in and out of all the women he could find who were thin and full of purpose and drew him into their bodies purposefully and without sighing.

I waited for him to come back. Whenever he came home, I said nothing but wondered only when he would come back to me or if he would ever come back. And for a while, after he found Sheila, I thought he would leave me and take all his things and I would never see him again unless we happened to meet by chance in the street. Because he fell in love with Sheila. He told me in a pub on a summer evening that he had stopped caring for everything in the world, even for his co-respondents and his ambition to be Cartier-Bresson, except the one, glorious, ecstatic act of putting his cock inside Sheila and letting his love pour out of him and into her, and he knew that unless he could do this day after day, evening and morning, he would go mad. "You must let me go, Ruby," he said and I could smell the privet hedge that bordered the little pub courtyard and I thought, all of London is held in that sad smell of privet and now after all these years I shall be alone in it. I looked at Leon and said: "Tell me about Sheila," thinking to myself, if only I could learn to be more like them, these women that Leon craves to love. But he wouldn't talk about Sheila, as if she was a thing too private and too precious to be talked of, but only said again: "You must let me go."

I knew that Leon would go then. There was no question of my letting him or not letting him: he would simply pack and go, which he did the following day. The same night Grandma Constad, who was alive then in 1969, but whose store of years had been so filled with her raging that I had come to believe they were running out, turned up at the flat.

"Ruby," she said, "you are a child of the Inquisition and none of us have ever thought about this enough and now you are being punished! The sins of the fathers, you see dear . . ."

I offered her some whisky, a drink she had taken to rather heavily and which did her no good at all, but made her say idiotic things, and she took the drink and said: "Why are you not weeping, Ruby? You have lost my son!"

"Leon will come back," I said to Grandma Constad. I said it quietly, not really believing it and she didn't hear it, but began talking about her own marriage.

"Ben was never unfaithful to me!" she announced, "because there was *union*, you see, Ruby. And how can there ever be union between a Jew and a Roman Catholic? There never can be. Leon should have married into his own kind and we would never have had to suffer all these troubles. I'm not saying I'm not angry with Leon, Ruby. It's his fault as much as yours. You see, I warned him at the time of your marriage, 'You will never have union, Leon not with a marriage like this!' "

Grandma Constad died a few months after this. She died while Leon was still away with Sheila, so that I didn't know of her death until I walked past her house one afternoon and saw all the curtains drawn and found that I couldn't help but hope that she had gone, because I never loved her. I had never found pity in me for her poor beginnings, nor understanding for her rages. She was outside me.

Sheila now lives in Grandma Constad's house. Leon gave it to her as a lavish parting present, little Chelsea house for the neat body where he had lived and found paradise. He didn't seem able to go on with paradise very long after Grandma Constad died; he felt too weary for it. He came home. I thought then – just as I'm thinking now – I must love him better, I must try to get thin. But then there was this awful weariness of his which was so deep and silent that it emptied me of all resolution. I thought it would stay with him for ever and that he had come home not to be with me again, but only to sleep. And

55

when at last he began waking up and his energy returned, I found that I had become a snail again, fat still, unlovable in most of my ways and offering nothing more than I had offered him on the day he went away and found paradise.

Sheila is still Leon's secretary. She sent carnations to the hospital. She still lives in Grandma Constad's house, and until he became ill, I think Leon used to go round there once in a while. I'm not certain about this and Leon and I have never mentioned it, but I only think it probable because in all the years since Grandma Constad's death and Leon's return, we have loved very little and very poorly and how could a man like Leon be content with a love that is so little and so poor?

At the Convent School, they told me: "There is only one love and this is the love of Our Lord, His for us, ours for Him." But not even then when I weighed twelve stone and saw and heard so little in my home that resembled love (our house was bathed in my mother's sighs; they drifted into every room) no, not even then, Sister, did I believe this. Because what on earth was the point of all those young poets opening their casements and looking out and feeling their hearts leaping like larks with joy or wilting like unwatered basil with sorrow if the love they leapt or wilted for wasn't a real kind of love but a sham, a thing only experienced by a few nervous young men who were destined to die of consumption or mosquito bites? The hours we stayed, Sister Benedicta, pondering this other love, the kind of love that Godmother Louise felt for Max Reiter and he for her, a love that I have wanted to feel ever since I sat in your room and thought, let me stay beyond sundown, and you never did. Those hours were quite in vain, Sister, when you have hidden your body and protected your soul all your life for the love of God and I have walked as if bandaged up for fifty years, never daring to take off the bandages and look at myself – wound or no wound – and let myself love. It's too late now. I have become so used to half-loving, it's all I can do. But when I go to the nursing home and stare at Leon, I sometimes think, damn all my

56

beginnings, damn the creeping nuns with their guilt and silences, damn the great white wall of the Convent School that girded the daughters of the high-ranking officers and kept out a continent and damn you, Sister, who only gave me a kiss like a benediction and never held me so that I could feel you and understand.

Alexandra dared – *tried* – to love. She dared to let Sue take her and bring her body to little ecstasies. She felt no guilt about loving Sue. She let Sue's love flame over her like a sunrise. And when Noel arrived, shouting soldier in the midst of her calm, she began to move, that was all, just slip very slowly out of the sunrise that had been Sue into the hard mid-day that was Noel. Sue saw her moving away. She watched and was amazed. Sue couldn't believe, loving Alexandra as she did, that she would just walk away. Sue followed and questioned. She pulled Alexandra back to her and shouted, "No!" But Alexandra slipped out of her arms like a child from a grown-up embrace and wandered in a kind of bewilderment towards her brother. The soldier in Noel was shouting orders: his sister must not love a woman. A woman! Because he found Sue and Alexandra together one morning in the very act of loving. He had woken early and wanted to talk to Alexandra. He opened her door and there was his sister, naked and hot with Sue's long scroll of a tongue bringing her to a perfect climax. "I'm good, Alexandra," Sue had said, and so Alexandra let it be and they were together for more than a year, happy and guiltless until Noel arrived and parted them.

For part them he must, he at once decided – only for Alex's own good, of course, for what would her life become, sleeping face to face with a woman far from anywhere until they were both old and their breasts sagged under the weight of each other's hands? And Alexandra found it impossible to send Noel away. She began to believe that Noel's arrival was meant "because I never really loved Sue and one day I would have gone away from her and never come back." Sue pleaded with

Alexandra: "Send him away, my darling. Please make him go."
But Alexandra said no, she couldn't send him away, he was her
brother and Christmas was coming on. She felt angry with Sue
because of the pleading and wanted to say to her: "You knew I
wouldn't stay for ever, Sue. I'll never love women the way you
love them. Loving women is a nice game." And it would have
been kinder to Sue, I often feel, if Alexandra had said this, but
as it was she said nothing about their love coming to an end, but
stayed quite silent, even letting Sue come to her bed night after
night and never pushed her away until it was Christmas Day
and the soldier, whose head was filled with rage, began his
march.

Alexandra told me that it turned very cold on Christmas
morning. She had spent the previous night in Sue's bed but
woke up to find herself alone. It was seven o'clock and dark and
the cottage was quite silent. Alexandra lay and waited for Sue to
come back from the bathroom or wherever she was, looked
forward to being warm with Sue for an hour or two before they
got up, lit the fire and had their Christmas breakfast and opened
their presents. She dozed, despite the cold, woke up again, saw
day beginning at the window and felt afraid. She got up and
went to the bathroom, then looked in her own room and stood
on the stairs listening for sounds. She could hear Noel snoring
by the burnt-out fire. Nothing else. No sound of anyone in the
kitchen making breakfast, no sounds at all but the sounds of the
morning beginning now, the hens murmuring and a church bell
tolling early Communion. She went back to Sue's room and
drew the curtains. The morning was whitening from its dawn
blue. There was ice on the window, frost on the little patch of
grass. Occasionally, Sue got up early and went out to feed the
hens, but no footprints marked the frosted grass, no sign of Sue
with her little basin of corn.

Alexandra sighed. She got dressed, thinking as she pulled
on her jerseys and thick socks, Sue will come back and I must
try to make this day happy – for us all. We'll build a bigger,

hotter fire than we've ever had! The sun was up now, slanting across the garden. She went to the window, opened it, and took a breath of the winter morning. There wasn't a sign in Norfolk of the rain that was falling on London. There, the day was frozen and bright, waking to its own perfection, like the first day of the world.

It's a very long time, Sister, since I remembered all this – or pictured it, as Alexandra once asked me to do on the one and only time she ever talked about it – and I feel tired now at the thought of that day's beginning and can't write down any more. You see, I must be full of strength today and not fail Leon again by walking out of his room without doing my Black Power salute. Because the days are going by and why is there no change in Leon, in spite of all my prayers and the fragile candles and the nurses coming and going and the eternal smell of flowers?

December 20

I keep trying to telephone Gerald Tibbs. I fear he may be away because his telephone is never answered. I imagine him passing through France on a train with his litre of wine bought at the station buffet at Boulogne and a glass smuggled out of the station buffet, cheap, round-bowled wineglass that goes with him all the way across France towards Italy and the wife who left him. I wonder about his children left behind, wise teenagers saying to each other: "Why is he so stupid as to try and find her? She's been gone more than a year now and never writes to us, not even cards on our birthdays, so why doesn't he just accept the loss of her and get on with his life?"

I have been trying to ring Gerald to apologize for my neglect of him. Since Leon's illness, you see Sister, I haven't felt I could go on helping him and though he's never written to me saying "What good is this, helping me for a while and then one day disappearing and never seeing me again?" I know he must be *feeling* "what good is this?" and I would like the chance to explain to him what has happened and why I can't help anybody at all, not even him of whom I had really grown quite fond.

During the time that I was helping him, I occasionally wrote bits of poems about him, starting with the poem about his wife going to Milan with her smart young man. I never showed the poems to Gerald, but one day, if he ever comes right out of his mourning, I might show them to him. The second poem went like this:

> Gerald has a begging bowl
> and with this bowl he begs
> for sympathy, not money,
> as if he were a bear who begged
> perpetually for honey.

Not that Gerald resembles a bear at all, so the imagery in this poem isn't at all good. In fact, it's really extremely misleading because Gerald Tibbs is a very white, hairless man with no hint of fur anywhere on his body and he treads the world with such a light step that he makes no mark, whereas bears are heavy and look as if they are constantly trampling things to death. Gerald actually looks a bit as if he had been trampled to death, or put into a dark cupboard for decades where no light has reached him, and you can easily imagine that after Gerald, the Romeo person, so brown and flashy, was like colour television after years with black and white. And after this there was no going back, not even for the furs, though perhaps she thought of them sometimes when it snowed in Milan.

I do hope Gerald isn't on a train in France with a stolen wine-glass, heading for a chemical factory and another explosion of sorrow from which he will surely never recover and it will take years and years to piece him together again. I wish he would answer his telephone so that I could say: "Gerald, for heaven's sake don't go rushing through Europe!" But he doesn't answer and I haven't seen him since the autumn when Alexandra came back from France, not even once to explain my silence.

It was soon after Christmas Day last year when he was sick in the bathroom that I rang him up. I rang him because I had never seen anyone in my life (except a middle-aged Indian woman in Delhi whose baby had been run over by a tram) so distracted with sorrow. He couldn't make a single gesture, a single little movement without revealing his sorrow in all its horrible shape and I thought, this demon of sorrow inside him will drive him mad unless someone begins to rescue him.

At first he didn't answer his telephone – just as he isn't answering now – but I kept on trying and trying until the day when he answered in his reedy voice and I said: "Gerald, I've been thinking about you a lot and daren't ask you if your wife has come back because I don't suppose she has." To which he said nothing, so I knew that she was still in Milan (which is the greyest of Italian cities and a bad choice if you are English and imagine all of Italy a-shimmer with olive trees and white with marble) and that Gerald was alone with his almost grown-up children and a house full of sad belongings. Gerald didn't sound at all pleased to hear me; he wanted to be left alone with his demon. But for once in my life I believed that I was right and that Gerald needed help. "I'd like to come and see you, Gerald," I said, "or you could come and see me if you like and I could cook you lunch, although I'm not a good cook at all as Leon's always telling me."

"Why do you want to see me?" asked Gerald and I could tell that he was very suspicious of me, thinking either that I had some bad news for him or that I wanted to rape him.

"Oh don't sound so alarmed, Gerald!" I said, "It's not bad news or rape or anything at all other than a feeling that no one was helping you much, in fact they seem to be hindering you really, taking you out to cocktail parties, and I thought, a nice plain lunch and a chat about whatever you liked . . ."

"I don't talk much," said Gerald.

"No, I know you don't and I don't as a rule, so we could have lunch in total silence, if you wanted to. I wouldn't mind at all!"

Gerald laughed. Laughter seemed to fill his voice and body out a bit.

"I'd like you to come and see me, Gerald," I said rather earnestly, "I'd love to know about your children because mine are grown up and miles away and I've forgotten how teenagers are. I mean, it's not even the Beatles any more, is it, it's other extraordinary Punk things with names like 'Cow Pat' and you sometimes wonder if it's not all a dance of death."

"Yes," said Gerald and coughed.

He did come to lunch. And it was during the first of the lunches that I had with Gerald that I discovered an extraordinary thing about him – he was a solicitor! It was idiotic of me to be so surprised because of course London is chock-a-block with solicitors, all of them quite different from each other. But it did seem very difficult to believe that Gerald's being wouldn't have

62

absolutely rejected the solicitor in itself like bodies reject transplanted organs, preferring to die rather than house a stranger, even for a few months. The notion that Gerald would ever be rung up in the middle of the night by a co-respondent in Beverly Hills was absurd. In fact, I'm sure none of Gerald's clients ever rang him up in the middle of the night, sensing that, being so pale, he needed a lot of sleep. So I concluded that he was in quite a different category from Leon when it came to solicitors, a category that I had never come across in all my years as a solicitor's wife and therefore found very hard to believe in.

For something to say (because Gerald is, as he warned me, a man of very few words and will surely die one day of terminal silence) I began to ask him about his work.

"At least you have your work, Gerald," I said, "and I have always envied people who were involved in a job." But Gerald didn't want to talk about his work.

"I'm fed up with it," he said. "I've got far too many cases. I can't give any of them my attention. My secretary brings all the files in and puts the on my desk. Toffee for a man with no teeth! I don't even start on them. I dictate stalling letters – 'You will be hearing from Mr Tibbs in the near future.' Near future! I don't believe in the future, near or far."

I had made a chicken salad for Gerald with bits of celery and nuts in it. It was rather dry food and this seemed to suit him because he picked and picked at it until his plate was empty and I remembered that at the Hazlehurst's dinner party he'd eaten nothing at all.

"Well done!" I said, when Gerald had finished his helping "You've eaten it all up!" And then I thought with shame, why do I treat him like a child? Why don't I know how to begin to help him? He looked at me crossly and I knew I was deservedly punished.

I got up, feeling very hot and uncomfortable and began to clear away the plates and the dish of salad, thinking that's the very worst thing I could have done, pat him on the back as if he was a five-year-old struggling with bread and butter pudding, the very worst, because he must be feeling like a child, deserted and helpless. I walked around him in silence, clearing the table. He sipped at his water (he had refused wine) and I knew that I had been no help to him at all.

He left very soon after this, saying he had to get back to his office.

"The lunch was most enjoyable," he said, holding out his hand to me, and I thought, oh the lies we tell in the name of good manners! And then he was gone, slipping silently away and back to his mound of files and the letters he wrote full of promises he'd never keep because his life was in tatters and I had just added to the store of those who had failed him.

Several weeks passed before I decided to try again. When I heard his thin voice answer the telephone, I dreaded saying my name, imagining that he would be utterly dismayed at the sound of it, but at once he began to apologize, saying: "I should have written, just a note even, I should have written to thank you for the lunch."

"Oh no, Gerald!" I said relieved, "it was a terrible lunch and I think I should have written to you really. You see, I was brought up in India, Gerald, and I'm afraid I've never quite lost it, the habit of never saying anything that's helpful. No one in India seemed to have a feeling for helpfulness, only a feeling for what is *right*, and it took me a long time to see that almost everything they thought was right was actually not all that right, but in fact rather wrong. And this deficiency in helpfulness, I mean, I've had it all my life and I blame India, but who can say if it was India or if it wasn't born in me, because it's a long time since India now and thank goodness all those feelings of *rightness* have been swept away . . ."

"If you were ringing to ask me to lunch again," Gerald said quietly, "I'd love to come. You were right about no one helping. They don't."

So he came round the next week. Over a rather tasteless

lamb casserole, which he didn't seem to enjoy and I didn't either, he began to knead away, gently at first, then more firmly, at his own misery until the pain of the kneading doubled him up and he began to cry. He kept apologizing, through his tears, for this crying, but it seemed to me that if you can cry over lunch with a fat woman you hardly know, then your need to cry is probably very strong and your tears might feel like a balm. So I said: "Oh no, Gerald, you're quite wrong to apologize. Don't even try to stop crying. Cry as much as you like."

"You can't imagine," he said at last, "what it's like to lose someone you knew was all you ever wanted. All, you see. I used to think, she's one of the wonders of the world, my Sarah. You can't imagine what it's like to lose one of the wonders of the world, to lose her in a single day!"

"Well, I can't Gerald, I know. But I can try. I mean, I know if anything happened to Leon – not that he's a wonder of the world, far from it really with his co-respondents and everything – I'd feel dreadfully lost. I don't know how I'd take root again. I might never."

"I never will ," wept Gerald, "I shall never be strong or patient or anything at all for the children. I feel I can't give them anything and of course it's terrible for them too, to lose a mother."

"I'd say they might be your salvation, Gerald. I mean, they love you, don't they, and you love them."

"I feel as if I love no one any more. Not even the children. I feel as if I was born just to love one person."

Gerald blew his nose and dabbed at his eyes. Between his elbows, his helping of lamb casserole was congealing. I felt empty of words, but wanted to put my arm round Gerald, imagining that since Sarah had left, no one had touched him. But then I remembered that because I am fat I sweat quite a lot and I thought, my heavy sweating arm will disgust him and he will want to tear out of the flat and never come back, thinking, even longing to cry and not crying is better than that,

65

if that's the price. I stayed motionless and Gerald, getting no more help from me, no word or movement, faded back into silence and very soon left.

That night Leon went out to dinner with a client and I got into bed early, not bothering to make myself a meal and glad that I wasn't in the restaurant with Leon and his client and their bottles of wine and glasses of brandy and cigars. I lay back in a clean nightie, having bathed and powdered my body so that there was no trace of sweat on it, and after a while thought up one of my poems about Gerald which went like this:

Today for the first time
Gerald wept.
I've never heard him weep before
But now I know
that while the world's been weeping,
I have slept.

There is more to say, Sister, about my comforting of Gerald Tibbs, but I feel tired out by the thought of him at the moment and, although it's very late, feel I must put down what happened today when I went to see Leon.

On the bus going up Oxford Street (I've given up taxis now, they're so expensive) I decided that in case I got faint-hearted again about doing my Black Power salute after spending an hour with Leon, I would do it as soon as I entered his room. I marched down the long, polished corridor to Leon's bower (actually, it isn't quite such a bower now as some of the flowers have died, including those intended for the ocean liner), went in as usual without knocking, raised my clenched fist into the air and shouted: "Come on, man! Come on, Leon, you've got to start fighting just like an oppressed person, Leon! You've got to fight for your right to live!" But there was a shriek of terror from the bed and a dying stranger shot bolt upright in the bed, a woman with a bandaged, shaved head dribbling fear and fumbling for the bell they told her she could ring any time, day or night, and nurses would come running. So nurses did come running and they pushed me out of the way with rough hands and dived on to the patient, laying her down, taking her pulse, soothing her and then turned accusingly to me and said: "What on earth are you doing here, Mrs Constad, when this patient is extremely ill and you know it's against hospital rules for anyone to shout like that and I think we ought to send for Matron at once because visiting can be limited, you know, and who do you think will be held responsible if this patient succumbs . . . ?"

So Leon had been moved. He hadn't died in the night without a murmur as I feared for a few minutes, they had simply wheeled him to another room because, Matron announced to me, "he is out of danger". OUT OF DANGER! Yes, they needed his old room for this new bald woman who was very much in danger just as Leon had been for nearly two weeks, but now, miraculously, the danger was past; he would not die.

I sat down on a bench in one of the shiny corridors and thought about this: Leon would not die. Matron had pronounced. Matron could not be wrong. I thought of the candles in the Oratory. How many more candles till he came crawling, creeping out of his chrysalis of silence and darkness? Had he perhaps begun to creep already and this is why they had decided "he is out of danger"? No, I couldn't believe this because only yesterday (even though the tubes are gone now and he is fed slops and sweet tea through his mouth) he had seemed more inert than ever, more lost in the spaces of his mind so that it was impossible to believe that anything but resurrection could bring him back from the seas he sailed because they were lost seas and no one would ever find them.

I tried to find one of the doctors. (India taught me that only men and nuns knew the truth and that ordinary women wove gossamer lies into their underclothes, enough to last a lifetime.) But all the nursing home could come up with was a very young Indian doctor who gave me a careful smile and apologized.

"I don't know your husband's case," he said, "I'm very

67

sorry but I'm not familiar with this case. But if Matron says he is out of danger, then he is. Be quite comforted."

I walked very slowly towards Leon's new room. I didn't feel happy about him being in a new room when I had known my way blindfold to the old one and it had always been in that room that I imagined him saying his first word. What would become of him in a new room? Would the nurses still come and go all day, making sure that he lived, or would they leave him alone for hour after hour, saying to themselves "he is out of danger and others need us more." Would Leon still have his own night nurse or only her empty chair for company and lie wondering, where has she gone with her little busy hands?

The Indian doctor had told me that Leon was in room 34. I found it and knocked – I was afraid to stumble on another bandaged stranger and learn the wrath of Matron – but there wasn't a sound from inside the room, so I opened the door slowly and quietly and went in. Leon was lying, just as usual, on his back and yet looked quite changed. He had been changed by the light. The whole of the room and Leon in it was bright with sunlight. He was lying in a pool of sunlight. I stared at him and felt sick. The light was terrible, a degradation. He looked poisoned by the yellow light. "Oh Leon!" I whispered, "what have they done to you?" I began to walk to the window and draw the venetian blind, but the nausea in me rose and rose and I stumbled to Leon's washbasin and vomited into it and soon after (I didn't glance at Leon again) a young nurse found me and said: "Oh Lord, dear, please come out of this patient's room and we'll find a toilet." I held on to the nurse's arm which was very cool and we seemed to slide along the shiny corridor and go sliding and sliding for miles until I was dizzy with all the sliding and I fell, tumbling over and over into darkness.

They can't stand Nuisances in hospitals. They see all visitors as potential Nuisances, taking up precious time by walking the wrong way down corridors and asking to be redirected like Arab women in Harrods who mumble incomprehensible questions about Lingerie and Soft Furnishings from deepest purdah and get on everyone's nerves. Most hated of all are visitors who are sick or who faint in corridors, and when I came floating up from my green unconsciousness, I knew that at all costs I must apologize to the nurse with the cold arm and to the Indian doctor, whose familiar face I could now see above me. But I seemed quite unable to form the words of an apology. It was like a maths equation that I couldn't do and never would and I found that all I could say was: "Leon's face. You mustn't leave it open like that." To which, quite reasonably, they said nothing, only told me to keep my head down and I would soon be better.

They called me a taxi. They didn't mention the sunlight or the sick in the basin, but only wanted to be rid of me so that they could go rushing about their millions of tasks undisturbed. I was too weak and too afraid of them and of being a Nuisance to say what I wanted to say, or even to get out my apology, which was lost somewhere inside me. I rode home in silence and, going down Park Lane, fell fast asleep.

DECEMBER 19

"When Jesus went into the garden of Gethsemane," you used to say, Sister, "He was dreadfully afraid. 'Let this cup pass from me,' he said. And because Jesus knew fear," so you said, "He doesn't feel ashamed of us when we're afraid. He doesn't say to Himself, 'What a hopeless cowardly person and let them be cast out for ever from my love.' Rather, He prays for us, and if we believe this, then we shall find strength."

Well, I keep going to the Oratory, Sister. I fold myself into the proper attitude of prayer and I think of Jesus at nightfall in Gethsemane and of His understanding after He had felt fear. I try to imagine Him praying for me, turning to God the Father and whispering: "Ruby Constad is afraid." It does no good, Sister. And now it is three days since I've been to the nursing home. Three days and my fear of the nursing home is so strong that I don't know how I shall get there ever again, unless there is someone to lead me like a child and go in front of me into Leon's room and draw down the blind and turn on the dim electric light.

This morning, I walked to Harrods' flower department, thinking to myself, if I buy flowers to take to Leon's room, then I will go to the nursing home. Because all of his other flowers must be dead by now – unless Sheila has kept on with her carnations – and I wouldn't like to think of Leon's room quite empty and colourless. I bought a bunch of daffodils. I think they must be Australian daffodils, because the cold is so biting in England just now that I can't imagine them growing any-where else but on the other side of the world (and anyway, Harrods is always full of extraordinary out-of-season things like Libyan strawberries in November and Tasmanian leeks in June, it's as if they believe no one in London should have to go a single week of the year without a leek or a strawberry, and this makes you realize that at heart Harrods is very stupid, like a magnificent gilded elephant with a tiny brain).

I intended to walk to the bus stop with my Australian daffodils and go straight to the nursing home. But I didn't do this. It was a very clear morning, with London brittle and bright in winter sunlight, and a clean blue sky above Sloane Street. It is almost the shortest day. By half past three it would be dark and all the sun gone and I thought, I'll go then. I'll go at four or five or even later, when Leon's blind is down.

But instead of walking home, I got on the underground and rode the Northern Line to Highgate, where the sky was still cloudless, and I walked very slowly to the cemetery. At one of the furthest corners of it, is Godmother Louise's grave. It is an uncared-for mound with a very small headstone that says only "Louise Reiter, 1901–1961" and no one passing it would know that for hundreds of days poor Max had come and stared at it and gone home again with the musician inside him bruised so badly by his sorrow that he composed nothing more in his lifetime and lived like a lame crab in a little hole, forgetting each day to write down the one thing he wanted to say – that he wanted to be buried by Louise – forgetting until it was too late and his Austrian relatives claimed his famous person and he was buried in Vienna.

I used to go and see him. He sacked the cook-housekeeper when Louise died and the house began to smell of dust and rotting food and cigar ends. I tidied up for him sometimes, but he preferred me to sit by him in the faded sitting-room where I had first met Leon and hold his long, white hand and listen to him grieving. "I'd rather clean and dust," I always wanted to say, "than sit so still and listen to your grief that will never end." "But I like it when you sit with me, Ruby," he used to say, "no one else sits with me. They don't want to listen."

Godmother Louise had been sixty when she died. She died unexpectedly, one day graceful and full of laughter and still reaching for Max's hand if they sat together on a sofa, and the next day yellowed by the certainty of death, which took root as a

71

cancer in her thyroid gland and sent her to her grave in Highgate in a matter of weeks. It seemed to me very unkind that Godmother Louise should die at sixty when she so loved her life "that I cherish every hour of it, Ruby, and never want it to end", when in St John's Wood alone, there must have been hundreds of men and women clinging wearily to their seventies and eighties, full of disgust and meanness, their bodies squeezed dry of life and love like old water-skins. Why couldn't one of them have gone and not Louise? So Max Reiter asked himself countless times as he sat and brooded on her memory, listening now and then for a snatch of music inside himself and hearing nothing, only the great silence she had created by dying and which would never again be filled.

I unwrapped my Australian daffodils intended for Leon and scattered them on Godmother Louise's mound.

"I shall insist that she goes to Highgate!" Max had said, "She was a good Marxist," and he had made a huge bureaucratic fuss to slip her emaciated body into its little corner of this most famous of cemeteries. I remember that at her funeral, I pondered the idea of Godmother Louise being "a good Marxist" and found it rather strange. I think I decided that she was only a good Marxist deep down in her soul and that she let the rest of herself be rather a bad Marxist. And the bad Marxist in her kept on and on going to five-star hotel rooms where enormous bouquets arrived "courtesy of the management" and where she sipped away, guiltless, at the finest champagne a bourgeois capitalist society can produce.

At least she had been right about India. Her loathing for the idea of empire had been as strong as Queen Victoria's love of it. She despised my parents for their snobbishness and their loveless ways. It was a kind of sickness, she said, their terrible pride and reserve, and I must be cured of it. I must forget the school for the daughters of the high-ranking officers, no longer think of myself as a daughter of a high-ranking officer, or even as a Catholic, because these were the masks to hide behind and until I threw them away, these masks, threw them away and never put them on again, I wouldn't know myself.

"This is why so many of us are lost, Ruby," she said, "this is why your mother and father are so lost: they are crouching down behind their masks; they believe they *are* their masks and without them they will be nothing!"

Godmother Louise had a very gentle but clear voice. I remember much of what she said because of that voice of hers and when she died, I missed it. It was as if a little fountain where I had often gone to drink had suddenly dried up, like the healing waters of Streatham dried up and there is nothing left to remember them by except the tiny pump house, and the traffic and the ugly high street buildings roar and thrive, ignorant that here was once a spring where people came to sip and be healed. Today, at the cemetery, I longed for the wisdom of Godmother Louise who surely would have laughed at my superstitious candles and my half-remembered prayers. She would have led me quite differently through this time and I would have followed, just as I followed her when I was young and married a Jew as she had done and thought so mistakenly, now my life will be like hers – a thing of beauty.

I was very hungry after my walk to the cemetery, and in Highgate village I found one of those all-purpose restaurants run by Italians, where you can have cups of tea and slices of battenburg cake or spaghetti bolognese at almost any time of the day or night, and where you find people having lunch at eleven and tea at two and dinner at one in the morning and no one seems to mind or even notice and the cooks in the basement go patiently on, resting for only a few hours and waking again to make cannelloni for breakfast.

I ordered chicken cacciatora and a glass of red wine. I rather enjoyed the meal out. I enjoyed being in Highgate, high up and away from Knightsbridge. I sat at my table until after three o'clock, ordering a second glass of wine and following this with three cups of coffee. I was waiting for the darkening afternoon to creep on. I thought of the sunlight slanting over Leon's bed, imagined it disappearing and the room becoming shadowy. I knew I was still afraid, but Louise had helped a little. The Australian daffodils were gone, so I would have to go to Leon empty-handed. This, of course, doesn't really matter when tomorrow I could take Rhodesian sunflowers or gardenias grown in a solarium on Mont Blanc.

DECEMBER 21

I was too tired after my visit to Leon yesterday to write about it, so I never told you, Sister, how it has increased my general confusion.

I went prepared to talk to Leon about the Wainwright case, thinking, it's time he wrote something else down and the mention of Richard Wainwright may jog his mind to make a pattern. But when I arrived at the nursing home, the receptionist popped quickly out of her booth and said:

"I wonder if you'd mind waiting, Mrs Constad. There is a visitor with your husband and we only allow one visitor at a time. If you'd care to have a seat?"

"What visitor?" I asked. "Who is the visitor?"

"I'm afraid I don't know, Mrs Constad. I wasn't here when she came in. I was advised by Matron to ask you to wait – if you came today."

"Well, surely it wouldn't matter if I went in? I wouldn't disturb Leon."

"Nursing home rules, Mrs Constad," the receptionist said with a smile. "We don't have many rules, but this is one."

She showed me to a leather chair in a room I'd never noticed before. It resembled a dentist's waiting-room: blackish oil paintings hung on damask walls, a polished table piled up with copies of *Vogue* and *Homes and Gardens*. I fell into the leather chair and stared at the room. I felt unbalanced by the news of Leon's visitor, rather shocked. I decided at first that the visitor was Sheila and searched myself for signs of anger. I found a little; I thought of the girl's body, imagined Leon telling her each day how he wanted to love it for ever. But then the anger passed. Leon's love for Sheila had diminished, died even, and I thought poor girl, when she sees him it will be a terrible shock, like seeing a dead person, and who knows if she won't feel like throwing up in the washbasin.

I got up and crossed to the polished table, deciding to pass

75

the time with a glossy magazine and not think about Sheila. I sat down with *Vogue*, which is inevitably crammed with photographs of thin women and Scandinavian kitchens and very bad therapy if you are fifty and fat and the London dirt gets into every cranny of your rooms and the plants on the kitchen window-sill die one after the other and you never know why. Looking at all the pages of expensive clothes, I thought, how strange when Leon has let me be rich that I've never been smart. Leon would have liked a well-dressed person for a wife and has now and then complained about my utter lack of smartness. If Leon gets better, I heard myself think, I shall try to smarten up – and I shall get thin. But then the thought of going back to India slipped suddenly into my mind. I saw myself walking, walking through a crowded bazaar, wearing some kind of robe that was loose and comfortable in the heat and which wasn't at all smart but made me forget my Western body crammed into its corset. I walked on, moving slowly with the crowd, a part of the crowd, going nowhere, only letting myself hear and see, full of wonder at the strangeness of the place and the people pressed in so tightly all around me, knowing that if I walked for long enough, I would be changed by what I saw and smelt and understood and my old ways would fall off me like scabs.

I put down the magazine and closed my eyes. No sooner were they closed than the receptionist came into the room and announced to me that I could go and see Leon now if I wanted to.

"What about the other visitor?" I asked.

"She's just left, Mrs Constad."

"I didn't see her go."

"No? She was quite a young person, wearing a duffle coat."

This was confusing. Somehow, I couldn't imagine Sheila wearing a duffle coat, not even in December on a dark afternoon.

"Are you sure it was a duffle coat?" I persisted.

"Oh yes. Black, I think. Though I couldn't say for certain. So many visitors come and go past me."

I walked slowly to Leon's room. I was aware that I had begun to wonder if the visitor hadn't been Alexandra. I had written to her twice, telling her that Leon's chances of recovery were good, but never asking her to come and see him, afraid that if he saw her, the great anger he had felt with her and with Noel would come rumbling up from inside him again and burst out of him in appalling incoherent noises. It had seemed to me better that Alexandra and Noel stayed away. In time, if he recovered, Leon might find that all his anger had gone and that he could think of them again just as he'd thought of them for more than twenty years – with pride and with love – and one day, he'd get down the photograph albums and chuckle with pleasure over the trudges up Snowdon in the mist and the picnics in France.

The thought that Alexandra was in London was a cruel one. Would she leave after her visit to Leon, just take the next train out of Liverpool Street, or would she decide to come and see me and stay a few days so that I would have some company and to tell me about her life? I knew that I was hoping desperately to see her and I knew that this was very foolish of me and that really I should have been wiser than that.

When I went into Leon's room, I saw that they had propped him up a bit and his right eye was wide open, staring fixedly at a chrysanthemum plant on a table near the end of his bed.

"Leon," I said quietly and to my surprise he turned his head a little and looked at me. I smiled at him, wished I had come with the Australian daffodils so that I could hold them out to him.

"How are you today, dear?" I began as I often begin. And it was then that a sound came out of Leon's mouth, a little breathless sound, the very first he has made since he had his stroke.

"Go on, Leon," I said, standing still in the middle of the

77

room, and with a great effort of concentration he made his mouth move again and another noise escaped it, tuneless, meaningless but there, and with it a little dribble of saliva that ran down his chin.

I took a handkerchief out of my crocodile handbag, went to Leon and wiped the dribble away. Then I sat on the bed and took his hand, watching his face for any sign of another noise. But he seemed to have given up and was content just to stare at me.

"I hear you had another visitor today, Leon," I said, carefully jollying my voice along. "I expect she brought you that lovely chrysanthemum plant, dear, didn't she? But I do wonder who she was, Leon. Because no one comes except me, do they? I can't think who it could have been unless it was . . ." I was going to say Alexandra and then thought better of it. I didn't know what the sound of her name might do to him. But it was at that moment that Leon pulled his right hand free of mine, reached for the slate and began to write in his slow shaky hand. It took him a long time to write the one word that was on his mind, but he finished it eventually and pushed the slate towards me. He had written "tomorrow".

I didn't know what he meant, Sister. I simply looked at the word and nodded and after that I didn't stay very much longer. With the afternoon being so dark outside the blind, I suddenly had the notion that after my visit to Highgate and my lunch in the Italian café and my wait in the leather armchair, it had grown terribly late and that in writing "tomorrow" Leon was saying he was too tired to see me and wanted me gone.

CHRISTMAS EVE

I've done nothing about Christmas this year. No dyed teasels in
Grandma Constad's hideous vase, no wreath on the front door
of the flat. And I've asked no one round. I would have invited
Gerald Tibbs, but still his telephone doesn't answer and each
day I feel more and more certain that he's in Milan by now,
lying dead in a gutter, his white face carved up by a broken
chianti bottle, and I bitterly regret that I didn't warn him, beg
him not to go before it was too late.

For a few months, I tried to help Gerald, first of all by
listening to him and letting him cry and then by daring to hold
him, feeling him resent me at first and want to push me away,
and then after a while coming nearer to me and lying with his
head on my shoulder.

This happened one rather sunny afternoon on the sofa in the
drawing-room after one of my badly-cooked lunches. It was just
a feeling I had that all the awful lunches were doing no good at
all, that Gerald would come and go and toy with the revolting
bits of food I gave him and wander off in his helpless way, his
burden of misery intact.

So I lay down on the sofa and said to Gerald: "Before you go,
Gerald, come and lie down, just for a few minutes, and let me
put my arms around you," and he looked at me horrorstruck, as
if he had been asked to lie in the jaws of a great white shark.

"Please, Gerald," I said, and I held out my hand to him.
"Please do it just for a second. You can forget about me, who I
am, all that rubbish. Just think of me as a raft, something to
hold on to."

"Ruby," he said, "I can't make love any more. I've tried."

"I'm not talking about making love, Gerald, I'm just talking
about letting me hold you."

He crossed to the sofa and clambered on to it. He looked
very apprehensive. The sofa wasn't very wide, so he had to lie
close to me. Feeling his thin body, I thought, he's like a stick

79

and one day he'll just snap, a brittle stick in solicitor's clothes, he'll snap inside his clothes and nobody will see. We lay in abject silence, but after a while, Gerald put an arm round me.

"You smell very nice, Ruby," he said sadly.

The following day, he telephoned me. "I couldn't sleep last night, Ruby," he said, "I thought about you all night, I'm so glad I touched you. I didn't really want to, but when I did, I was glad."

I said nothing. Really, I felt like laughing, but I didn't want Gerald to think I was laughing at him.

"Are you there, Ruby?" he asked worriedly.

"Yes, I'm there, Gerald."

"I'm awfully tired," he said, "not having slept at all, and I was wondering if there was any chance . . . if I could come round for an hour or two and just lie with you and sleep?"

I thought of lying with Gerald on the bed I shared with Leon, and rejected the idea. But both Alexandra and Noel were away and I supposed we could lie in Alexandra's room, on a single bed under the shelf of ornaments which had been there since she was a little child.

"Yes, Gerald, do come round. Leon went to America this morning," I added.

I suppose I never should have told Gerald that Leon was away. Then he would have had his little doze and thanked me and gone home at about four or back to his office to write more letters of apology to clients he would never see. But as it was, he slept for three hours and, waking up to find me beside him, decided that his private Waterloo had arrived and he had to find out now if he could do it or if Sarah's leaving him had made him impotent for ever.

He took out his cock, which was small and white like the rest of him, but quite erect, and after a lot of fumbling with my corsets and pants simply slipped it into me. He held on to me as if he was drowning, quite without tenderness or affection, but biting his lip in a terrible desperation. I hardly dared move, in case his tiny sex slipped out of me and he couldn't get it in again. It took him a very long time to come and in all his exertions he never looked at me or kissed me, but stared straight at the wall, at a fixed point on the wall until the moment when he knew he could come and he pressed his cheek against mine with a little sob of relief as the sperm shot out of him for the first time in weeks and months and he knew that he was still a man. His Waterloo past, he was silent. Then a few minutes later he sprang off me with a bound and said: "I'm going to put the kettle on, Ruby. I'm parched!"

I lay on Alexandra's bed and wondered why I had so wanted to help Gerald and whether I had helped him enough now and could give up. I couldn't construe what I had done as unfaithfulness to Leon, because there had been no passion in it and for me not even a second's pleasure (not that Leon regarded the notion of faithfulness as anything but "Victorian rubbish", and this presumably included me as well as him) but it hadn't been very enjoyable to lie like a shipwreck under a drowning man, and now that the drowning man was safe and wouldn't die, I wanted to be free of him. I fastened up my corset with a sigh.

But I went on being the shipwreck. Occasionally, the drowning man – sensing, perhaps, that he was out of danger – gave me a little attention, kissing me and putting his trembling hand on my big breasts. But after a few times, I understood why his wife Sarah had run off with her olive-skinned Romeo. Gerald had never discovered that a woman could feel pleasure too and longed to feel it, and if you had told him this he would have felt a terrible sense of impropriety and probably run away. I went on being the shipwreck, about once a fortnight, until Alexandra came back from France. Then, a terrible feeling of guilt appeared inside me and I telephoned Gerald at his office one morning and told him curtly never to come back. And for a while, I forgot him completely, never giving him a thought or wondering if I had hurt his feelings, never asking myself, how will he get on without my body to take pity on his infantile sex?

81

Until quite recently, when the year has crept towards Christmas again and I have begun to remember how he was the evening he was sick in the lavatory, quite defeated by his sorrow.

I feel very ashamed, Sister, about everything that happened with Gerald. Ashamed of what I did and of what I failed to do. I marvel sometimes that all my years have never taught me to be wise and it serves me right, I dare say, that now I'm alone with myself and it's Christmas Eve, Christmas Eve even in California where the day is just beginning and Leon's co-respondents have all their gift-wrapped presents hidden away with their shoe trees. None of them will give Leon a thought, nor a thought for London which is deserted now except for tourists in big hotels and rubbish flying about in the wind and little posses of beery youths sicking up into alleyways.

Like Leon last year, when Noel didn't arrive, I long for Christmas to be over. I keep thinking that there may be a knock at the door and it will be Alexandra in the duffle coat described by the hospital receptionist, but really I should give up all hope of this. If it was Alexandra at the nursing home, she must have gone straight back to Norfolk, and this isn't surprising because after last year's Christmas, she must want to make amends to Sue (if indeed Sue is there and hasn't gone off with a girl who loved her better). Since Alexandra went back to the cottage in the autumn, she hasn't written to me, so who can say what has happened? Only in my dreams do I ever get to the cottage, but I know that really I shall never go, having promised Alexandra that I would stay away and not go near her until she asked for me.

I am writing now with a martini beside me and half a shaker full of it in the fridge – a little Christmas Eve treat to myself – and perhaps if I drink it all, I shall wobble my way to bed and sleep right through Christmas and when I wake up the M4 and M1 and the A12 will be bathed in a cloud of exhaust fumes, as all the Londoners fart their way home from their country weekends with boots full of broken plastic toys, saying "Thank

82

God that's over for another year," exactly as Leon said after his day in bed with the albums, "Thank God that's over," and then put on his suit and went back to the office.

What Leon didn't know that day was that nothing at all was over, not even his disappointment in Noel, but that it had just begun, begun then and there on Christmas morning when Alexandra woke early and looked for Sue and couldn't find her. Long before Alexandra looked out of the window and took her breath of the winter morning, Sue had crept out of the house and in the pitch darkness started her moped and ridden away. A note scribbled in crayon and left on the kitchen table said: "See you next term. Please feed the hens. Love, Sue."

Alexandra made a mug of tea and sat on her own in the kitchen, warming her hands on her mug and staring at Sue's note. She felt bewildered. She hadn't asked Noel to the cottage, didn't really want him there. Now Sue had gone and her present for Sue – an oil painting of Sue she had done secretly from a photograph – would stay wrapped in the garage and instead she would spend all the hours of Christmas with Noel, eating food that Sue had bought. She felt like a thief. Some of the voices she heard inside her as she sat there with her tea blamed Sue with her sulking and jealousy, but others told her: "You should have sent Noel away. You've been weak and unkind to Sue and it will be weeks before you'll be forgiven and can be at peace again with Sue and the hens and the routine of the cottage."

When Noel got up, always a bit frozen and cramped by his nights in the sleeping-bag, and wandered into the kitchen with his cheerful "happy Christmas, Alex!" all Alexandra could say, without looking at him, was: "Sue's gone."

He sat down on the other side of the table and held out his hand to Alexandra. "Cheer up," he said, "the world is full of Sues." And Alexandra, suddenly enraged by him, hurled her tea at his face, missed it narrowly but deluged his crumpled pyjamas. The hot tea stung but didn't burn. Noel swore and

83

stamped off to the bathroom, leaving Alexandra to mop the floor.

This was the beginning of that Christmas Day, Sister, as Alexandra described it to me. She told me that the rest of the day, until the evening, was very quiet. Alexandra sulked as she prepared the turkey Sue had got from a local farmer; Noel lit the fire and sat reading by it. The sunshine melted the frost on the garden and went down and almost at once there was a frost in the air again. Alexandra felt hungry and cold and wanted to be by the fire, but stayed in the kitchen, drinking tea and waiting for the food to be ready, but forgetting to feed the hens even though Sue had put their little basin of corn by the back door.

When the turkey was at last cooked, Alexandra piled all the food on to trays, opened a bottle of wine and shouted to Noel to come and carry them into the sitting-room. They squatted down by the fire and spread the feast all around them. Noel rubbed his hands, glad that the silent day with its tolling of church bells and freezing afternoon was coming to an end, and careful now to be nice to his sister, to make amends. The food warmed and cheered Alexandra; she felt her body revive and her guilt begin to leave her. Sue will have gone to friends, she decided, she'll be alright with friends, or even with her parents in King's Lynn, who would have cooked a magnificent meal . . .

When they had eaten two helpings of the turkey, Noel produced a present for Alexandra. It was a glossy book of Magritte paintings and Alexandra marvelled over it as she touched it, was suddenly very glad that Noel had given her something that she liked so much. "I've got nothing for you, Noel," she said, "I thought we'd agreed – no presents." Noel shrugged. He pretended not to mind, finding he did mind. He opened another bottle of wine, uncurled himself on the floor and took sip after sip. He felt rejected.

Alexandra cleared away the food, put on some music, and

84

came and sat near Noel and looked at the Magritte paintings. But Noel wanted her attention and made her put the book down. He began to ask her about Sue, asked her gently this time why she had tied herself to Sue. "Don't you like it with men?" he said and Alexandra shrugged her shoulders.

"It's OK," she said, "but they're so selfish." So Noel began to talk about his loving of Christine, describing it, saying he didn't believe any kind of homosexual love could compare with what a man and a woman could have together, if they understood each other's bodies and the perfection of giving and taking.

"He talked and talked about it," Alexandra told me, "he was turning himself on, trying to blot out Christine by seeing me as a challenge. And I knew in the end – I'd half known it ever since he arrived – that he'd just smother me with himself and I wouldn't resist. In fact, I knew that I wanted it, that I'd make him offer it all."

By the time Noel touched Alexandra, beginning with her black hair, then stroking her face and neck, and then pulling her slowly towards him, she was on fire for him, thinking over and over to herself, this is why he came here and in the end it's beautiful and perfect and I have loved him all my life. And the image of Sue speeding off into the darkness on her little bike never entered her mind again. All she whispered when she woke up the next day with Noel beside her was: "My life has changed", and she laughed.

So this is where it began, Sister. I imagine a hundred-year-old judge banging down his mallet with an age-flecked hand and wheezing out the word: *Incest*. I see you shudder under your grey gown and cross your arms to protect yourself.

I have almost finished the martini . . .

CHRISTMAS DAY

Last night, before I sailed off to sleep on my martini sea, I lay blinking at my dark room and thought up one of my poems. I'm not sure if it's about Leon or about Gerald, but I don't think this matters; making up poems, like writing letters to you, Sister Benedicta, who will never read it, seems to keep my mind alive. Without the letter and the mediocre poems I believe I might have lost myself and started to wander about London in a daze with a suitcase crammed full of stolen Marks and Spencer's knitwear and Jubilee Souvenir tea towels, until the heavy hand of the law reached out and tapped me on the shoulder and I was hauled up before the magistrate with not a word to say for myself.

The poem I wrote last night went:

> I wish I could have been a ship
> and sailed the seas I've never known;
> instead, I am a shipwreck
> and all who sail in me will drown.

Very soon after that, I drowned myself in my martini sleep and to my surprise it was rather a happy drowning which I didn't regret at all, because I expected to feel very sorry for myself today and in fact I don't feel too bad at all, only relieved that Christmas Day has come at last; I'm living it now, minute by minute (even though it's only 10.30 in the morning and there's a long way to go yet) and when I wake tomorrow morning, it will be over.

I'm rather worried that the vermouth bottle won't last until the shops open again. It's so long since I had a martini that I have quite lost the habit (so important when Leon was here) of checking the drink supply. However, yesterday's drizzle has left off; the sun seems to come and go, so I may wander out later in search of a little Off Licence that has dared to sneak up an "Open" sign for an hour or two. London seems to have quite a lot of these and they function in the same spirit as the round-the-clock Italian restaurants, not defying convention exactly, but ignoring it.

I think if I had a good supply of martini to last the next few days, I would feel much more cheerful that I've done for some time. I don't know why I've never thought of getting drunk before. If I was a man I believe I would have thought of it and gone stumbling and shrieking along the Victoria Embankment or flown off to Venice for a few days to snivel in cafés by the foul green canals, hopeful for a warm girl on a cold street corner or a good cry at dawn in a shabby hotel room. As it is, all I have done is sit and wait. I have stayed close to Leon, tried to become close to God, waited patiently for Alexandra to come and see me, and all three are mute! Only I have talked on silently to you, Sister, and where am I now but perched still in this tired flat, just serving out my time.

I have never before spent Christmas Day quite by myself. In India, we sometimes sat down twenty to the table decorated with scarlet and gold crackers shipped from Fortnum's to match the scarlet and gold uniforms of all the soldiers, and my mother would let a pale smile cross her face at the sight of so much finery, because she loved the army better than anything in the world, better than my father, who was only a tiny part of the army, and better even than Wiltshire where she had begun her life and for which she often mourned. "A soldier's bride!" she once exclaimed to me in a rare moment of delight, "When I knew I was to be a soldier's bride, I went out into the garden and sang 'Land of Hope and Glory' by the lily pond!" (Whenever I hear this tune now – which happily isn't often – I imagine my mother singing it in her Wiltshire garden and the old gardener, Len, hearing her and thinking, Lord love us, she's gone nutty.) And I've always known, from the day she told me about singing "Land of Hope and Glory" because she was so full of pride and joy, that she only married my father because he was a soldier and not for love of him. I think any officer would have done, but

87

who can say if she would have sighed more or less with someone else? I can't believe that she would ever have been happy, unless the entire British Army (Other Ranks excepted) had made her its mascot and cleaved itself only unto her.

When India was over and we moved to London, I very soon began to betray my parents by refusing to follow them on trains from Paddington down to the dusty house in Wiltshire for Christmas, where my thin grandmother sat blinking in an armchair all day, dying of indolence and memories and deaf as a post, so that if ever you plucked up your courage to interrupt her blinking with a word, she'd turn on you accusingly and shout: "Write it down, dear!" And a little notebook would be shoved into your hand into which you scribbled the most terrible trivia like: "You're looking extremely well, Granny," or "Did you have much trouble with greenfly this summer?", to which she seldom replied except with an enigmatic nod. She was the most unloving of grandmothers, a palsied version of my mother, who smelt rather nasty because she was to lazy to wash herself and who quite often wet her knickers and the faded silk cushion covers without any shame at all, only remarking with her perfectly-formed vowel sounds: "Oh look, I've done one of my puddlies!" and ringing her bell for the long-suffering housekeeper to come and take the cushion away. I couldn't stand the sight or smell of her, nor the Catholic in her which had transformed her room into a dusty shrine, but had never broadened her heart. Christmas at her house was like an internment: the world was shut out and all I could think of was the day when we would get back on to the train and I would discover it again in all its loud complexity.

I don't know how many such sad Christmases I endured in that house with its lily pond (an apologetically foul place by the time I saw it so that it was very hard to imagine anyone wanting to sing by it, let alone such a rousing number as "Land of Hope and Glory"), it wasn't more than three or four and after that I forgot my grandmother just as if she had died and went each year, in defiance of my mother, to Godmother Louise's house, actually sleeping there for the duration of Christmas, in a cold top room which the Reiters always referred to as "Ruby's room". Max chose to see Christmas as a day invented by the world in honour of Louise. He filled it with flowers and champagne and presents and his own music, "which never really got going in me, Ruby, till I met Louise". His joy in all this giving was ecstatic and by the time the evening came and the inevitable friends arrived and friends of friends and the goose was roasted ("In Vienna we used to eat goose and this is much nicer that turkey, Ruby, which was invented by the Americans") his little bearded person seemed to be on fire with happiness and we sat down to the candlelit meal like excited children, thinking, no other Christmas will ever be as wonderful as this.

Leon and I spent one Christmas with the Reiters before we had Noel, in the same little top room, reaching for each other in the early morning cold and making love until the house woke up and we could smell breakfast and hear Max singing in his bath. We *did* love then, I remind myself, when Leon had his office over the Fleet Street gym and we lived in a small flat five minutes walk from Hampstead Heath.

Before lunch that Christmas Day, Max and Leon and I went for a walk on Primrose Hill. It was windy and very cold and on the way home we all linked arms and ran stumbling and laughing, our cheeks bright with cold, our three breaths puffing out like steam along the empty streets, running home to Louise, quiet and beautiful in her flower-filled room to listen to Max play for an hour while we sipped champagne and waited for lunch. If I could have stopped time just once in my life, I would have stopped it there that morning on Primrose Hill, with Leon and Max holding my arms and giggling like boys.

Now time seems to have stopped here. London, so full of laughter that one Christmas morning, has gone silent. I imagine the little scufflings of countless old people, balanced on the edge of their lives in the tenement buildings that still criss-cross

London with their concrete balconies and their dark stairwells, the comings and goings of lives lived out by ancient gas fires, tea in brown pots, bits of chuck steak fried in dripping, "just enough for one, dear, don't give me any more than I can afford, because I won't have company, not this Christmas, and food's too dear to waste . . ." I wait and listen and come and go as they come and go, but they are thin and shadow-eyed on their pensioners' diets and all my life I have been wasteful and fat.

The telephone was ringing when I got back from my visit to Leon. It was Gerald. As it turns out, he *has* been rushing across Europe, but not to Milan, thank goodness, (of which he made no mention at all) but to some smart ski resort in Austria with his two children and flying down mountains with uncharacteristic enthusiasm and little daubs of colour in his cheeks.

"Ski-ing, Gerald!" I echoed.

"Yes. It was dreadfully expensive. You couldn't move – up or down the mountain – without paying, and cups of hot chocolate were a pound."

"They couldn't have been, Gerald."

"Yes, they were. I had to call a halt to hot chocolate after the first week."

"Well, no wonder!"

I was very relieved to hear Gerald's familiar voice. My image of him bleeding to death in a Milan cul-de-sac had been quite strong at times. But now he sounded very much alive, chirpy even, as if he'd got on much better without me and his strivings on Alexandra's bed, and the apology I was going to make for my desertion of him seemed superfluous.

"Well," I said, "it's nice to know you've had a holiday, Gerald."

"Yes, I feel much better, and Ruby . . . after all your, well, kindness to me last year, I'd like you to be the first to hear my news!"

"News, Gerald?"

"Yes. I'm getting married again."

I sat down, taking the telephone with me and tripping over the wire as I went. I was quite lost for a word, as if it was my turn to go in a board game and I had suddenly lost track of the rules.

"Married?" I gaped.

"Yes. She's called Davina."

My first thought was, we must wall up Italy! Let no men out and no-one called Davina in!

It seemed incredible to me that any woman could commit herself to Gerald, knowing him as I did, little white panting man with a broken heart. And I couldn't but believe that it was only a matter of time before Davina went the way of Sarah and then what would become of Gerald? I wanted to say: "Don't do it, Gerald. Don't ever fall in love again, you poor stick of a man, let alone marry!" I saw the whole dreadful process begin again, and by the time Davina left him, he would be old and impotent then for ever and crumble away to nothing inside his pinstripes.

"That's wonderful news!" I eventually stammered out, "Wonderful news for Christmas Day!"

"Yes, well I hope you and Leon will come to the wedding, Ruby. It'll be in the spring."

"I will of course, Gerald, but—"

"Oh yes. I heard from someone that Leon's been ill. I hope that's all over and done with."

I paused. I didn't want to taint Gerald's little spasm of joy with my long miseries.

"He's getting on," I said.

"Oh good. Well, you tell him that whatever happens, he must be OK by April 1st."

"That's the great day, is it?"

"Yes. Davina's choice."

Gerald wanted to fix a date for us all to meet and go out to a restaurant, but I told him that until Leon was better I couldn't really do this.

"I hope it will be soon, Gerald," I said, and he seemed

content with this, said Happy Christmas two or three times and rang off.

Once his voice had gone, I closed my eyes. "God weeps when we are foolish," you once said, Sister. So I took God's role upon me for a moment or two and shed a long tear that ran slowly down my face and on to my skirt. I didn't weep for long, any more than God does, I dare say, at our individual follies, but saves his great rivers of tears for the terrible stupidity of nations and lets them fall as rain on the fields of Flanders or on the plumes of the Viceroy in Anglo-India. Perhaps the British weather is, and always has been, a sign of God's sorrow at our idiocy and it has gone on getting worse ever since the Charge of the Light Brigade and the Battle of the Somme and the invention of Lord Birkenhead, and no wonder the Thames is angry and brown and the American tourists all arrive with plastic hats in their raincoat pockets.

Leon was crying when I got to the hospital this afternoon. What I didn't fully realize – and the doctors hadn't pointed this out to me – is that because the whole of his left side is paralysed, he can't see out of his left eye, not being able to raise this eyelid. And if you sit on the left side of the bed, he can't see you, unless he turns himself round to look at you, and this is difficult and uncomfortable for him. Today, he wanted to tell me to move round to his right side, making gestures with his right arm that I failed at first to interpret, thinking he was trying to show me something in the room. And because he wasn't understood, he began to weep, making very odd sounds out of the corner of his mouth and letting his eyes, which are puffy already, fill and refill with tears.

The nursing home has been gaudily decorated for Christmas. They hung a last year's paper chain above Leon's window and I wondered if all the colours in it haven't added to his sorrow and made him wonder what on earth is Christmas doing here in a sickroom and where's my son, whom I waited for last year and have never seen again?

92

Leon took the slate after a while, still crying, and wrote: "I can't see you." And it was then that I understood about his left eye, so I moved round the bed and sat very close to him on the other side, taking his hand and stroking it, but making no attempt to stop him crying. In the middle of his little noises and his slow tears, there was a tap at the door and Matron strode in, crisp and powerful and full of "glad tidings", so she said.

"We're getting him up tomorrow, Mrs Constad," she announced, "his blood pressure's responding very well to treatment, so it's time he was up."

I stared at Matron and then back at Leon, who was wiping his eyes on his pyjama sleeve. I imagined his thin legs under the covers.

"Isn't it too early for that?" I questioned.

"Oh no! We've got to have him active again, haven't we?"

"He won't be able to stand, will he?"

"Well, only on one leg – like the flamingoes I saw in Tanzania! And even that one will be a bit wobbly. But he'll be supported of course, and we'll only go a little way down the corridor to start with."

"Won't he be frightened of walking?"

"Oh, a little. It won't last long. He'll begin to feel happier about himself once he gets going."

Matron looked at me sternly. "It'll be a long path, Mrs Constad. Hours of patience. But our rehabilitation unit is one of the best in the country and your husband is really quite young – young enough to recover."

Then she sailed out and I was left staring at Leon, who had stopped crying and had shut his eyes, as if all this talk about rehabilitation had tired him out and he wanted to sleep.

"Well, Leon," I whispered, "I hope you'll be alright, darling. You hang on to the nurses and they won't let you fall."

Leon opened his eye and looked at me and began to struggle with some gurgling sounds in his throat that sounded a bit like Chinese on a far-away radio. I watched and waited, in case a miraculous piece of an English word might find its way out of him, but after a minute or two both he and I knew that it wouldn't and despairingly, he reached for the slate again, crossed out "I can't see you" and wrote: "bring Noel".

His writing has got much stronger since that day when he wrote "the night nurse masturbates'", but today I felt for the first time that my long vigil over him has made me weaker than I was in those first few days when I thought he would die. I seem to have very few resources left for him, ever since the day I was sick in the basin and began to feel afraid of the nursing home, and hardly any words left. So I felt angry with this sudden order, remembering that in all my years with Leon, he has never ceased to give commands and that I have never ceased to follow and guiltily aware that though I didn't want to lose him, I have been rather glad of his enforced silence.

I got up and walked to the window. I heard a taxi pull up, meter still ticking, and wished I was in it, running for home. With my back to Leon, I said: "I can't bring Noel, dear. I haven't seen him for more than a year. As far as I know, he's still in France. I don't know how he's managing to live, when everything there's so expensive. I expect he's got a job selling the *New York Times* or the *Herald Tribune* to Americans in cafés. The Americans can still afford France. It's only us and the Italians who can't. Anyway, Leon, if Noel comes home, I will bring him to see you. He could give you a hand with your walks down the corridor."

I turned round. Leon was nodding; he seemed to have understood.

But now that I know for certain that Leon is thinking about Noel and wondering where he is, I feel worried that he won't let his mind rest, when no doubt it should be resting and not dragging heavy thoughts about like chains. Perhaps I shouldn't have told Leon that Noel has disappeared and that his body could be floating down the Rhône, for all I know. Perhaps I should have said: "Noel's back at Cambridge, Leon, and with

94

his innate understanding of the law, sailing on towards a first-class degree," and the great lie would have rallied him and made him try extraordinarily hard at his rehabilitation, bringing a scoutleader's smile to the lips of Matron. Our lives are full of such confusions: when to lie and when to say the truth (I love you; I love you not) and when to keep silent.

BOXING DAY

That's that, then. Christmas Day has come and gone. It is foggy everywhere according to the television weathermen and there will be multiple pile-ups on the motorways, despite the hazard warning lights and the mothers of dead children will say: "If only we'd stayed at home . . ."

The people in the flat next door are away and I hope they don't die trying to get back. I have become very used to their quiet "Good mornings" and their comings and goings with their rubbish. They are middle-aged and walk on tiptoe, never disturbing, never asking favours. You couldn't ask for better neighbours, and even their name – Smith – is very accommodating because it's so easy to remember, so that I can always say: "Good morning, Mrs Smith", or "Good evening, Mr Smith" and feel I'm being friendly. They, on the other hand, seem to find Constad rather difficult and seldom say it, knowing it's Jewish perhaps and being anti-Semitic at heart despite their silent good manners, or else remembering Grandma Constad lumbering up three flights of stairs one evening, walking by mistake into their open flat and panting:"Those bloody stairs. My God! Why on earth do you live so high up? Do you think it's clever or something to live so high up?"

I imagine the Smiths staying in a neat and tidy vicarage in the heart of Gloucestershire, putting on suits to go to early service, eating and drinking wisely, giving each other identical volurnes of John Betjeman's poetry for Christmas, going for walks in wellingtons, watching the Queen on television ("in her Jubilee year, dear, we *must*") and thinking the eternal, unspoken thought of all who live lives like these: I'm glad we're who we are.

DECEMBER 27

I wonder if there will come a day when I stop writing my letter, a day when I say to myself: "it's over, finished, that's the end of it", sign my name and imagine that I've sent it half way across the world to you, Sister, in the room where I always picture you? Of course I shall never send it. Not only because the India of your days is long gone and you are dying or dead in some English convent, but also because I'm afraid that what I've remembered about you over the years, you have long forgotten, and when it finally reached you, this big parcel of words, you would open it, turn it over and peer at it and say to yourself: "Who is this Ruby? I never knew her." To the little ghost of you that flutters now and then at the edges of my heart, I dedicate the rest of this letter. But I got no further with it yesterday because of this thought that in so many years of teaching the daughters of high-ranking officers, you never found the time to remember one. For they came and went like flowers and in our uniform we were all the same and hundreds of us, over the years, crept to your room to sip tea and discover Keats, and you took a little pride in us all, the ones who liked poetry, but not one more than another and you gave us all your mothwing kiss, your benediction.

I sat and pondered you, Sister. I imagined that you were the last of the nuns to leave the Convent School after it was closed, that you waited, waited in the empty, echoing building, thinking, it can't be true; they can't have taken the girls away and sent all the Sisters home to England after their years and years of devoted service. The Viceroy will come and he will remember the pageant, how we made "welcome" in girls for him and bowed our heads to the imperial person, yes the Viceroy will come with his hat and his medals and say, "It was only a dream, Sister Benedicta, only a terrible dream that they sent the girls away and put the nuns on boats bound for England; and tomorrow, you wait and see, they'll come back again and the servants will come with brooms and clean the building, chase away the lizards and the dry leaves, keep a watch out for cobras as they always did, and then you can come out of the corner where you sit and wait, put on a clean habit, wash your face that is white with dust. . . ." But the Viceroy didn't come, though you thought he might, day after day, and you waited a long time for him and even composed a letter to him in your head. The Viceroy didn't come and you knew after a while that he never would; so you crept out of the building, never giving it a backward glance, carrying your few belongings in an old leather suitcase. And only a day or two later, you walked up a gangplank of a ship bound for England with the great weight of India in your nun's heart – all that you'd known and all that you'd never dared to know.

When I got on to the ship that brought us home, my mother and me (my father would follow later with his regiment), and the harbour of Bombay began to slip away from us, my mother turned to me and said: "Well I'm glad it's over," just as if we were getting on a train at Brighton station after a fortnight's bad weather. She didn't shed tears, as I imagine you did, Sister, only turned her back on seventeen years of her life with a sigh identical to all the sighs that had drifted through our house ever since I was a tiny child and she had sighed as she put me off her knee.

She didn't go ashore at Aden or Cairo or Athens or even Gibraltar (which I felt sure would be abounding with British officers) but stayed in her cabin for most of the long journey, and as we crept round Spain and then up France and the weather became very cold, she began to remember all the disadvantages of England, such as the terrible difficulty of getting servants and the incontinent ways of my grandmother with whom we were going to live for a while, until my father came home to his job at the War Office and we found a house in London.

At Southampton, where it was raining, she sighed and

grumbled more than she'd ever done – grumbled about the dirt on the train windows and the slowness of our porter – till an old black taxi deposited us and our heavy luggage at my grandmother's door, when she sighed at last with relief that she'd arrived and said again: "Well, I'm not sorry that's over," and my grandmother came tottering to greet us, saying: "You're an hour late, you know," as if India was just up the road.

The first night in Wiltshire – in a room to myself at last – I kept my light on until very late and wrote to you, Sister. "England is awful now that we're going to stay here for ever," I wrote, "all I think about is the school and hope that all the Sisters are well." I wrote to you several times, I think, even once or twice after we moved to London and I came to know Godmother Louise and started forgetting my Catholic ways, and once you wrote back, saying: "Everything here is just as usual. Cook's boy, Shanker, found a king cobra in the pantry yesterday morning and told me he'd asked Jesus to help him kill it. I think we may have a convert, so Sister Angelina and myself offered up a prayer of thanksgiving in case we have!"

But not for long could you write: "Everything is just as usual." The years crept quickly by until the day, Sister, when there was silence all around you and not even a cook's boy to convert and you waited in your corner for the Viceroy to arrive and tell you it was all a dream.

DECEMBER 28

True to her word, Matron has had Leon out of bed these last two mornings. "I couldn't walk", he wrote on the slate today, and Matron told me in private that "as is absolutely normal," Leon was very upset by his first attempts to put his dangling useless leg to the ground and cried all the time. I wanted to say to her: "Please don't try any more, if it distresses him," but Matron put a comforting square hand on my wrist and said: "I hope Dr Woods warned you that during the period of recovery – and it *is* recovery, Mrs Constad, we're sure of this – stroke patients are always very emotional. They know there is a struggle ahead and they're experiencing a lot of confusion. They're very easily disappointed, made angry even, and this is why I said to you the other day: 'It's a long road back.' But with your patience, and ours, I honestly believe your husband will get completely well."

I asked Matron about Leon's talking, or rather his inability to get a word out and the terrible sideways struggling of his mouth. "Speech therapy," she announced, taking her hand off my wrist, "again a longish road. He will, in effect, have to learn to talk again."

I came out of Matron's office feeling very depressed at the thought of all the struggling Leon was going to have to do. He hates any process that goes slowly and is always trying to speed things up, even the process of the law, never learning in twenty-five years that the law cannot be hurried, just as Grandma Constad never seemed to learn things that were obvious and died quite ignorant of much that people with less cluttered memories learn in infancy.

I went back to Leon's room and sat down by him again. He looked puzzled to see me back, thinking I'd gone home. "I thought I'd pop back for a minute, Leon," I said, "I won't stay long, because it's very late and I get so cold going home. But I just wanted to say to you, you must try to be patient with this rehabilitating; think of it like riding a bicycle and don't imagine you can do it in a day. I mean, of course you can't walk, dear, not straightaway, but only by moving, so they say, will the life creep back into your leg and then you will walk."

I paused, in case Leon wanted to write something on the slate, but he didn't reach for it and was staring at me intently, so I went on.

"They're going to help you to talk again, Leon. They're going to send a speech therapist who will help you make words again; because the words are there inside you, dear, you haven't forgotten them, you just have to learn how to say them again. And Leon, it may not be so long before you can come home, and I'll do all I can to get you going. We'll work at it night and day. I mean, what else have I got to do but help you and it's all I think about, really, making you well."

I stopped talking and waited for Leon to nod or write something down, but he didn't, so I patted his hand which used to look brown all the year round and which has now faded to yellow, and walked slowly to the door, where I made a rather undynamic Black Power salute. He saw my salute this time and looked frightened to death, as if I was a Symbionese Liberationist about to kidnap him. So I brought my arm down, said gently: "See you tomorrow, dear," and left. At the moment, two nurses have to feed him: one to hold his mouth open and the other to spoon in the slops that keep him alive, and I thought on my way home from the hospital, if he does come home, how will I manage?

I haven't been to the Oratory since before Christmas so I decided to go there this evening, Sister, and light two candles – one for Leon and one for Noel, about whom I have become afraid and would dearly love to know, after all this time, that at least he's safe. I imagine him in Avignon, which was where Alexandra last saw him when she left him her mini – just gave it to him because he needed it and she didn't care about anything any more, not even about her car – and got on the sleeper for

101

Boulogne. Avignon: terrible crumbling old city with decay and tourists hammering at its heart. I hope Noel didn't linger on there, but went south again with the girl he met at the beach café, or took the Paris road and found work there. I prayed to Our Lady (who, in her forgiving way, surely intercedes with God for wayward children like Noel). I asked her to let him be safe and told her that my anger with him seems to be passing and that if he writes to me for money, I'll send it. "But best of all," I whispered, "let him come home, so that we can talk and I can take care of him for a while and then he can start again, take a new direction . . ." But even as I lit my candle, I remembered Alexandra saying: "He won't come home, not for a long time. He doesn't think of the family any more. He's glad he's hurt us. He wants to be far away and imagine our hurt."

She said all this in anger. She was crying when she said it, thinking of Noel with the girl he met at the beach café, so who can say if she was right, or if it was her anger talking and telling lies.

Alexandra wanted Noel to stay with her. She wanted to belong to him, be his. "I didn't mind," she said, "about people whispering and disapproving and saying 'brother and sister, how could they?' I loved Noel. I thought we'd stay together."

Noel did stay with her for a while. He lay with her in her cold room and forgot Christine and Cambridge, finding his sister's body that he hadn't looked at since they were children, miraculously beautiful. "We forgot about everyone else in the world," Alexandra said, "we forgot they existed. We didn't go out, except once to the pub to buy wine or just to bring in wood for the fire and feed the hens. We didn't even cook. We ate up the cold Christmas food. Sometimes we made up the fire and played music. Most of the time we stayed in bed. We couldn't let go of each other. We touched each other all the time. I'd never known that with anyone else, that wanting to touch them so badly."

The heavy frosts stayed and the new year came. Alexandra

eart, Sister, even when I'm on my knees or payin[g]
or a candle, I have kept on believing that sooner o[r]
before he's well and back at his office with th[e]
file on his desk, Leon is going to die.

told Noel he could stay with her as long as he liked, wanting him to stay for ever now that she'd found him, imagining them growing old in their brand-new love and believing that time wouldn't alter it. And when I think of this, I really wonder why so many hearts are sown with this sprig of illusion, when nothing is forever, as you found the day the Convent School went silent, Sister, and we should learn when we are children that the brightest sunrise is nothing but the prelude to nightfall.

In the first week of January, Sue came back. She arrived rather late one evening, looked at Alexandra and Noel and understood. She went to bed without a word. Alexandra felt uncomfortable with Sue's silence, wanting her either to be angry or forgive. Noel was sullen, loathing the silent presence of Sue in the next-door room and made love to Alexandra roughly and noisily, wanting to punish them both. Alexandra cried, knowing they couldn't live like that, the three of them, and wishing that Sue had stayed away. She wanted to shout to Sue through the thin wall: "You should have left when you did and never come back!" And she lay awake till dawn, listening to the two breaths that sighed through the darkness, Noel's beside her and Sue's on the other side of the wall.

"But in the end," Alexandra told me, "it was rather simple and surprising. Sue went off again the next day. She said she'd only come to get her things. She left quite early in a borrowed car and I was still in bed. I heard Noel saying goodbye to her, but Sue wouldn't say goodbye: she just got her things together and drove away. I wanted to explain to her what had happened, but then I thought, no, there's no need. Explanations are luxuries, and anyway Sue sees it all, there's nothing else to say.

"I let her go without seeing her and waited for Noel. I thought, now we shall get back to our standstill world. I needn't give anything else my attention, not even my work that I'd neglected since the day Noel arrived. I knew I couldn't work. I'd lost interest in it. I never thought Noel would go back to Cambridge. He told me he'd lost heart with Cambridge. But he didn't know what else to do. He saw my term at the art school beginning. He thought I'd be working all day and never be with him. So he just went. He said he'd ask Daddy to give him a car, so that he could come and see me at weekends. He promised to come for the whole of the Easter vac. and he said: 'In the summer, why don't we go abroad somewhere, perhaps to France, and not tell a soul where we are going?' "

By the end of January, then, Alexandra was alone. She wrote and told me that Sue had decided to "move on" and that now she was there on her own and two of the hens had died of cold and neglect. "Noel came for Christmas, as you already know," she added, "we had a nice time and now he's back at Cambridge."

When Leon read her letter he commented: "Of course Noel's back at Cambridge. Where else would he be in the middle of term?" And Leon and I didn't even know then that Christine had left Noel. I imagined him with Christine and wondered how glad he felt to be in bed again with her miraculous hair. I wondered if he would decide to marry Christine, and if so, how I would break the news to Leon.

Quite soon after getting Alexandra's letter Leon went to America and I began my poor adventure with Gerald Tibbs and the rain kept on in London and I now and then envied Leon in the California sunshine, drinking bourbon in the gigantic white houses of his co-respondents. I thought, why isn't my life more filled with colour? And if I was younger, like Sarah Tibbs, and had met an Italian, who knows if I wouldn't be in Italy now in this early springtime, watching the lemons turn yellow on the trees.

Leon came back from America very tired. Tired to death, he said. In the three weeks he was away, he put on almost a stone and his face looked very round, like his father's that I'd seen in faded photographs by Grandma Constad's bed. He was full of self-disgust at this new weight on his body that had always been thin and at the way he'd been made to live in

America, drinking at lunchtime, ⟨...⟩ not just a martini or two, but tu⟨...⟩ drinking far into each night, so t⟨...⟩ with a sour stomach and a headach⟨...⟩ imagine why you did all that drinkin⟨...⟩ it," he mumbled: "Part of the job ⟨...⟩ stand." And I wondered what else h⟨...⟩ if the marbled houses of Beverly Hi⟨...⟩ with plastic smiles, put on for the sn⟨...⟩ who spoke with not a trace of Li⟨...⟩ willingly drowned in the scented, pe⟨...⟩ be plundered and stained, and only ⟨...⟩ came home: "I'm tired to death."

I didn't ask Leon what he'd done i⟨...⟩ makes no difference, just as Gerald Ti⟨...⟩ just as long as Leon doesn't believe h⟨...⟩ and start spending all the money he⟨...⟩ telephone calls and flights to L.A. ⟨...⟩ paradise, because there were no flig⟨...⟩ (except from the co-respondents in th⟨...⟩ only a lot of worrying about his weight⟨...⟩ made up by Leon's private doctor which⟨...⟩ the things Leon hated most in this world⟨...⟩ radishes, so that Leon didn't follow the ⟨...⟩ clung to him, to his stomach and to his t⟨...⟩ never left him until he had his stroke. S⟨...⟩ stroke had nothing to do with what ha⟨...⟩ Alexandra that autumn and Leon's grea⟨...⟩ came about only because of those three w⟨...⟩ and if Leon is ever completely healed, ⟨...⟩ "Whatever you do, don't go back to A⟨...⟩ respondents come to you."

Suddenly I admire the bluster and stre⟨...⟩ thinks she can give Leon back his limbs an⟨...⟩ that, despite my size, there is no bluster and⟨...⟩

and in my ⟨...⟩
my money ⟨...⟩
later, long ⟨...⟩
Wainwrigh⟨...⟩

told Noel he could stay with her as long as he liked, wanting him to stay for ever now that she'd found him, imagining them growing old in their brand-new love and believing that time wouldn't alter it. And when I think of this, I really wonder why so many hearts are sown with this sprig of illusion, when nothing is forever, as you found the day the Convent School went silent, Sister, and we should learn when we are children that the brightest sunrise is nothing but the prelude to nightfall.

In the first week of January, Sue came back. She arrived rather late one evening, looked at Alexandra and Noel and understood. She went to bed without a word. Alexandra felt uncomfortable with Sue's silence, wanting her either to be angry or forgive. Noel was sullen, loathing the silent presence of Sue in the next-door room and made love to Alexandra roughly and noisily, wanting to punish them both. Alexandra cried, knowing they couldn't live like that, the three of them, and wishing that Sue had stayed away. She wanted to shout to Sue through the thin wall: "You should have left when you did and never come back!" And she lay awake till dawn, listening to the two breaths that sighed through the darkness, Noel's beside her and Sue's on the other side of the wall.

"But in the end," Alexandra told me, "it was rather simple and surprising. Sue went off again the next day. She said she'd only come to get her things. She left quite early in a borrowed car and I was still in bed. I heard Noel saying goodbye to her, but Sue wouldn't say goodbye: she just got her things together and drove away. I wanted to explain to her what had happened, but then I thought, no, there's no need. Explanations are luxuries, and anyway Sue sees it all, there's nothing else to say.

"I let her go without seeing her and waited for Noel. I thought, now we shall get back to our standstill world. I needn't give anything else my attention, not even my work that I'd neglected since the day Noel arrived. I knew I couldn't work. I'd lost interest in it. I never thought Noel would go back to Cambridge. He told me he'd lost heart with Cambridge. But he didn't know what else to do. He saw my term at the art school beginning. He thought I'd be working all day and never be with him. So he just went. He said he'd ask Daddy to give him a car, so that he could come and see me at weekends. He promised to come for the whole of the Easter vac. and he said: 'In the summer, why don't we go abroad somewhere, perhaps to France, and not tell a soul where we are going?' "

By the end of January, then, Alexandra was alone. She wrote and told me that Sue had decided to "move on" and that now she was there on her own and two of the hens had died of cold and neglect. "Noel came for Christmas, as you already know," she added, "we had a nice time and now he's back at Cambridge."

When Leon read her letter he commented: "Of course Noel's back at Cambridge. Where else would he be in the middle of term?" And Leon and I didn't even know then that Christine had left Noel. I imagined him with Christine and wondered how glad he felt to be in bed again with her miraculous hair. I wondered if he would decide to marry Christine, and if so, how I would break the news to Leon.

Quite soon after getting Alexandra's letter Leon went to America and I began my poor adventure with Gerald Tibbs and the rain kept on in London and I now and then envied Leon in the California sunshine, drinking bourbon in the gigantic white houses of his co-respondents. I thought, why isn't my life more filled with colour? And if I was younger, like Sarah Tibbs, and had met an Italian, who knows if I wouldn't be in Italy now in this early springtime, watching the lemons turn yellow on the trees.

Leon came back from America very tired. Tired to death, he said. In the three weeks he was away, he put on almost a stone and his face looked very round, like his father's that I'd seen in faded photographs by Grandma Constad's bed. He was full of self-disgust at this new weight on his body that had always been thin and at the way he'd been made to live in

America, drinking at lunchtime, drinking again at six o'clock, not just a martini or two, but tumblers full of whisky and drinking far into each night, so that every morning he woke with a sour stomach and a headache. And when I said: "I can't imagine why you did all that drinking, Leon, if you didn't enjoy it," he mumbled: "Part of the job Ruby. You wouldn't understand." And I wondered what else had been part of the job and if the marbled houses of Beverly Hills hadn't been decked out with plastic smiles, put on for the smart solicitor from London who spoke with not a trace of Liverpool in him, and who willingly drowned in the scented, perfect smiles and let himself be plundered and stained, and only mumbled when he at last came home: "I'm tired to death."

I didn't ask Leon what he'd done in California. I thought, it makes no difference, just as Gerald Tibbs makes no difference, just as long as Leon doesn't believe he's found paradise again and start spending all the money he earns on long-distance telephone calls and flights to L.A. I don't think he found paradise, because there were no flights or telephone calls (except from the co-respondents in the middle of the night), only a lot of worrying about his weight and a very idiotic diet made up by Leon's private doctor which seemed to consist of all the things Leon hated most in this world like cottage cheese and radishes, so that Leon didn't follow the diet and the extra stone clung to him, to his stomach and to his thighs and his face, and never left him until he had his stroke. Sometimes I think the stroke had nothing to do with what happened to Noel and Alexandra that autumn and Leon's great burst of anger, but came about only because of those three weeks in Beverly Hills, and if Leon is ever completely healed, I may say to him: "Whatever you do, don't go back to America. Let the co-respondents come to you."

Suddenly I admire the bluster and strength of Matron who thinks she can give Leon back his limbs and his voice. I realize that, despite my size, there is no bluster and strength in me at all and in my heart, Sister, even when I'm on my knees or paying my money for a candle, I have kept on believing that sooner or later, long before he's well and back at his office with the Wainwright file on his desk, Leon is going to die.

DECEMBER 29

Gerald Tibbs telephoned me again this morning.

"Davina and I would very much like you to come round for a meal," he said, "If Leon's still in hospital, I imagine you're jolly lonely. And it's not as if I've forgotten how you helped me when I was lonely, Ruby . . ."

"I think that's probably best forgotten, Gerald."

"Not at all! I was in a poor way, a very poor way and you—"

"That all seems a long time ago, Gerald, and now your life's really come on. You can put last winter firmly in the past."

"Oh I have, Ruby, I have."

"You mustn't feel you owe me anything, and really I'm quite alright on my own. I'm getting very used to it."

"But we'd like to see you. Davina hasn't met many of my friends yet because she's quite a shy person. It wouldn't be a social occasion. We're all agreed, aren't we, we don't like them very much? But we'd like to see you and we thought, if you haven't got any plans, what about New Year's Eve?"

I was silent. I found I couldn't hear Gerald's reedy voice now without imagining his white body going through its exertions on Alexandra's bed. I saw it for an instant, naked except for a paper hat, saying "Happy New Year, Ruby", and the paper hat which was orange fell off onto my face.

"I don't think I can come on New Year's Eve," I said, "I usually stay at the hospital until quite late . . ."

"The later the better, Ruby. It's miserable to start anything too early on New Year's Eve, don't you think?"

"Well, I know, but I'm not good company at the moment, Gerald. I may even have gone batty and not know it, because there's no one to tell me and I noticed on the tube going to Highgate that people looked at me oddly."

"Oh we'll tell you," Gerald joked, "if you've gone mad! Davina's expert at that kind of thing."

"But New Year's Eve, you see, everyone wearing hats . . . I don't think I could."

"It'll only be us, Ruby, just us. As I say, Davina is a very shy person, but I know you'd make her feel at home."

This was an extremely confusing thing for Gerald to say. He's muddled about everything, I thought, and sighed one of my mother's despairing sighs that echoed down the wires to Gerald who ignored it and said brightly: "New Year's Eve at about nine, then?"

I've never been to Gerald's house, which is quite big and grand in a Kensington square. I can't help wondering if the shy person, Davina, has taken out all the furs and dresses that cluttered the bedroom cupboards and carried them off to a jumble sale, or if Gerald himself threw them out when he felt his heart begin to mend, and Davina never saw them. I don't suppose I shall ever know the answer to this, unless Gerald himself should mention it in his New Year's Eve euphoria, in the shelter of his paper hat.

I'm not looking forward to going to Gerald's house or to meeting Davina. I would prefer to leave Gerald to tempt fate unseen. I've decided that I won't be at his Fool's Day wedding, and I hope that New Year's Eve will be the last time I see him, because he has no need of me now and must turn to people like Betty Hazlehurst who won't try to be to wise and will rejoice with him. I notice that I'm becoming a bit like my mother, very miserly with joy and quite unfit to attend weddings or celebrations of any kind, just as she was.

She came to my own wedding dressed in grey, only outdone by Grandma Constad, who draped her enormous frame in black lace and you would have thought from all the sighing and grumbling that came out of these two women on that day in 1949 that they were burying their children, not uniting them. And I couldn't help but think of my mother singing out her love for the British Army by the lily pond, and I wondered why, when I was a child of the British Army, she wouldn't sing for me.

She and Grandma Constad hardly spoke, but stared at each other like museum exhibits out of their widow's eyes, never met again as long as they lived, but remembered that terrible day all their lives, so they said, knowing the Faith had been betrayed. My grandmother who, in her damp old age, had outlived my father and might outlive us all, so once I thought, was carried up the steps of the London hotel in her wheelchair and was heard to shout at my mother as she entered the flower-filled room: "Is Ruby pregnant? Is that why she's got to marry this Jew?" And in my white dress, I wished her dead and wondered why she had to live on and on when the soul inside her skull seemed to be crawling with maggots.

Louise had chosen and paid for the flowers. My mother was just glad to be spared the expense and didn't listen when Louise said to her: "Max has always filled my life with flowers; I would like to fill this day for Ruby." Louise chose lilies, white roses, gardenias and scented stocks and when you entered the room where our few guests sat down to lunch, the smell of these flowers was like mid-day in Eden, and I made Leon ask the hotel management if we could take some with us on our boat to France, because I wanted to hold this Eden in my hands and make it last.

Leon and I had asked Max Reiter if he would play for us after lunch. The hotel had charged extra, my mother said, for getting a grand piano into the room. He played two Bach preludes and then a new piece of his own that he had composed for us and had called *Summer Song*. But my grandmother spoiled his playing by hiccuping very loudly all through it and then saying, near the end, "I've never liked this kind of thing. I'm told he's famous, but that doesn't mean anything these days, does it?" And I wondered why I had allowed my mother to bring this terrible old woman to my great day, to sit under her rug and spoil it and I felt ashamed of myself and of them both with their joyless eyes.

"I'm dreadfully sorry about Granny," I whispered to Max

afterwards, "she's quite decayed and terrible and I never should have let her in!"

He took my hand and said: "Ruby, I refuse even to mention your grandmother! She had her day long ago, but this one is yours."

"We love *Summer Song*, Max."

"Do you? Well, it was for you. Now you must see if you can make your summer last!"

It seems to me now that it lasted ten years, and by the time Louise died in 1960, it was over. For five of the ten years, Leon had his office above the gym in the Fleet Street alleyway and during this time, often said to me: "I'm biding my time, Ruby. It's very hard to become known in this business, but in a year or two . . ." And I thought, don't wish our lives away, Leon, don't live on and on for tomorrow and not sense the purpose of today.

I have a very old tape recording of Max's *Summer Song*, made before tape recorders were properly invented and I can't play it any more because Leon sold the big tape recorder some years ago as an antique to the Science Museum and bought a Japanese cassette machine instead. But I used to play it. I played it the night Louise died. I believe I thought it would remind me of Louise, of her laughter and her beautiful hair and her joy. But I found that I wasn't thinking about Louise. I was thinking about a day, a hot June day when Noel was at Miss Forester's school and I took Alexandra on to the heath in the early afternoon. Alexandra was three years old under her linen sunhat and the smell of her little body was like fresh cream. I sat her down beside me on our old rug, happy that the hot sun shone on us, that we were there with the familiar shapes of the heath around us and that Alexandra was mine. She lay down on her back with her legs in the air and looked at the blue above us, and I lay down beside her and shut my eyes. The sun on my face mocked my closed eyes, light crept through my lashes into my head and for a minute or more I forgot where I was. I've become

110

the sun, I thought, it's easy to become the sun! I must tell Leon and the Hazlehursts and everybody we know how easy it is to become the sun. I lay quite still. I dreamed I held in my head the light of continents, until a cloud crept in front of the sun and I sat up. I looked all around me, saw everything and yet nothing. A space. This was what I first noticed: there was a space where there shouldn't have been a space. Then I understood. Alexandra had gone.

I got up. I was no longer the light of all generations; I was ragged with terror. I was a beggar with nothing where once I had been rich beyond imagining. I ran this way and that, calling. I had no idea how long I had been lying down – two minutes, fifteen minutes? – and fears crowded into me until my calling became a scream and picnicking students and school-boys playing rounders and dog-owners of all ages heard it for miles around and I fancied the heath had gone strangely silent, sensing the inevitability of tragedy.

Alexandra heard my scream. From a little dell, where she had wandered to play, she came running to me and I lifted her into my arms and crushed her with the weight of my joy at finding her until she began to cry. She had been no more than ten yards away from me.

The dog-owners walked on, the students turned back to their sandwiches, the schoolboys started to bat and run, the sun came out again and I carried Alexandra to the rug and we both had a drink of lemonade from a thermos cup that tasted of stale tea. And it was then, holding the child's hand, that I knew that the sun's mysterious passage into my head was only a poor imagining and that what truly filled me was a sense of wonder at my life, at the love in it which seemed boundless and bright. I felt blessed, Sister. My body on the ground beside my child was never – before or since – as beautiful as it was on that day. I rocked Alexandra on my knee and found that in time to the rocking, I was humming Max's little piece of music. Alexandra laughed. I thought, I can't remember if I told Leon yesterday that I love him, but I shall tell him this evening, before he's put his latchkey down, I shall tell him that all my days are filled with love for him and for our children and this is how it will be until we are old and sit together in the silence of our rememberings.

I collected Noel from school and walking home with the two children, I knew that I never wanted to move from our little Hampstead flat, even though it was cluttered with the children's toys and Leon often said: "How can I bring clients here, to this mess?"

But then my mother died and left me the money she'd been so careful with all her life (even grudging our Indian servants the few rupees they earned to keep her idle and discontented) and we bought a house in Chelsea, not far from where Sheila lives now. In those days, Chelsea was rather a quiet place and even the fishmonger delivered to your door and a horse and cart selling flowers used to go up and down the King's Road, and sometimes the horse's hooves and the little cries of the flower-seller were the only sound.

Leon moved his office several times during the years we lived in Chelsea, first to Holborn, then to Bloomsbury and finally to Mayfair, which he's never left, only moved round it to bigger, grander offices as he took on partners and more and more rich clients who expected to see him in a large office and would quite have lost faith in him if they'd found him above the gym, with the squeaking and thudding of the apparatus going on all the time, even while they talked.

After Louise died and I made my visits to Max in the house in St John's Wood, he often said to me: "You're happy, aren't you, you and Leon?" And a year or two earlier, I would have answered "yes" and not been lying, and now I answered "yes" and knew that I was lying, remembering my autumn walks on the heath and thinking, it's slipped away from us since then, the kind of happiness that Max understands. And it wasn't very long after Max's death that Leon went secretly in search of paradise.

"He's getting on alright!" Matron said to me today, "I think he's begun to try, and that's half the battle."

When I went to see Leon, he was fast asleep and snoring like a very old man with his mouth open, tired out, it seemed, by his trying. I sat down by the bed and waited for him to wake up, and I thought of a remark my mother made to me one warm evening in India when my father had fallen asleep in his chair: "Never wake up a sleeping man, Ruby. If you do, he thinks you're offering yourself." And she said this with a shudder, as if the thought of offering her thin-waisted body to my father's wide one was like brushing her lips with death, and I wondered how many times in all her years with him she had offered it and where my father had gone in search of love, perhaps even to the officers' mess?

"Leon," I whispered, putting my face very close to his, and he opened his eyes and looked at me; or rather, he opened his right eye and the skin over the left eye hardly moved. Matron hasn't mentioned eye exercises, but he will surely need them, if he's to sit in his brown-carpeted office with a shred of his former dignity – though it's very hard to believe that he will sit there one day, buzzing for Sheila to take Mrs Wainwright away and bring in Charlton Heston, which was how he seemed to carry on before, when he looked at the world through both his eyes and manufactured all his quicksilver words that made him rich and known.

"Only me, dear," I said.

Leon was lying very far down in the bed and looked rather buried by it. I wanted to help him up. "Shall I help you up, Leon?" I asked, "or do you want to go back to sleep?"

He held out his right arm and I took this to be a sign that he wanted lifting. He was heavy to drag up on to the crumpled pillows. I wished I was Matron with her strength and her "years of experience of these sort of cases, Mrs Constad", and I did a very mediocre job of lifting Leon, so that he looked tilted and uncomfortable and I thought, why do I do everything so badly and by halves, like my healing of Gerald and my loving of Noel?

I stayed only a short time. I talked a little, and while I talked, Leon slid down the bed again, needing to rest, it seemed, to gather strength for the next day's walk down the corridor.

I told Leon that a new year was coming in a few days and we would at last be free of 1977, which had been the worst year of our lives, worse even than the freezing winter I spent in my grandmother's house in 1946 when never a day passed without someone grumbling out the word "rationing" and my cold room was the only refuge in a place gone sour with my grand-mother's leavings, the spilt sherry and the urine-stained cush-ions.

"I'm looking forward to next year," I told Leon. "It'll be a year of patching-up. You're on the mend now and let's try to mend everything that's broken in our lives."

Leon's eyes were closed. I think it's ages now since he's listened to a word I say, and even these days, when I'm his only visitor, he doesn't seem inclined to give me his attention for long. Or perhaps it's just this weariness of his, that Matron wants him to strive against, but which seems to come from deep inside him and if he could talk, he'd look at me each day as he looked at me when he came back from America and say: "I'm tired to death."

Before I left – as soon as I said I was leaving – Leon opened his good eye, reached for the slate and wrote: "bring the albums". There are eight albums and they are all extremely heavy, so I shall have to take them to the nursing home one by one, beginning chronologically with the pictures of me when we moved to Chelsea and Leon spent a month's earnings on his expensive camera and began to feel like Cartier-Bresson: me at thirty in a webbing belt and pleated skirt and white-rimmed sunglasses, when Noel and Alexandra were tiny children on kiddicars in our backyard garden. There are dozens of almost identical snaps of me smiling and holding one or other of the children, and it was only later on – in the third album, I think – that Leon noticed that many of the people in Cartier-Bresson's photographs aren't smiling at all, but in fact look full of tribulation and confusion. And from then on, he kept saying to me: "I don't know where you've got this idea of smiling from, Ruby. For heaven's sake take the smile off your face!" In consequence, in the last four or five of the albums I invariably look very glum, so that Grandma Constad once remarked: "Why does Ruby come out so terribly in your snaps, Leon?" And Leon, who hated his photographs to be called "snaps", snapped: "She's not photogenic, Mother. It's not my fault."

Once or twice, Leon let us all smile – in the cafés in Brittany in front of our Orangina bottles, or tobogganing on Wimbledon Common one snowy January Sunday. We smiled at the summit of Snowdon, but the clouds came down on our moment of triumph and we suddenly lost Leon and his camera who had only been a few feet away and our smiles vanished as we imagined him loosing his footing and plunging down the mountain to his death.

The last album is – or was – Leon's favourite, because at least half of this one is filled with pictures taken in Cambridge when he and Noel spent a weekend there "to get the feel of Cambridge, Noel" before the term began. It was August and very hot. The buildings look golden. Leon lay in a punt and photographed Noel as he punted. They sat in a pretty riverside pub and Noel photographed Leon whose skin had gone brown in a day, and he looks burnished with content in a strange floral shirt that he's never worn since because it reminds him of that day, one of the most perfect of his life.

I suppose it might be wisest to bring him the last album first and let him look at Noel. Ever since the day when he wrote "bring Noel" on the slate, I have wondered how he might react if Noel was suddenly brought back from the room in Avignon where I imagine him – cheap, musty room with grey lace at the window and a communal W.C. down the corridor – brought back as he is and not as Leon wanted him to be with his liking for pubs and his innate understanding of the law. No doubt Leon would weep, because he weeps at all things and can't stop himself which Matron says is quite normal and is to be expected for some time to come – but whether he would weep with anger or despair or joy if he woke up one afternoon and found Noel sitting by his bed, I'm unable to tell. I only remember that in the autumn, when Leon found out that Noel and Alexandra had been together in France and that Noel wasn't ever coming back to Cambridge to follow the path chosen for him, his Jewish rage came gushing out of him so violently that he seemed insane, but Noel who was in Avignon never saw it, only imagined it perhaps as he lingered on in France as the weather grew colder and he thought of the autumn term in Cambridge going by without him. Perhaps Leon's anger with Noel has just passed through him – as mine seems to be passing through me – and is gone without a trace, and if Noel did go to the hospital, Leon would shed tears on the hand he held and forget all about Cambridge and the weekend they had there, just the two of them, when the sun shone and his hopes for Noel were high.

To be safe, however, I think I shall start by bringing the first of the albums, because I don't think Leon could feel anger for children on kiddicars or playing on a windy beach in Wales, or indeed for me when I was young and still in the habit of smiling. And if he felt any nostalgia for those black and white faded days, he could comfort himself with the reminder that he's come a long way since then when his office was above the gym and his telephone was silent right through the night.

Then it occurs to me that Leon may only want the albums in order to tear them up, page by page, and send all those years flying into the hospital dustbins, wishing that he'd never tried to become Cartier-Bresson, when now the limit of his world is a few feet of corridor and his camera eye is closed. I don't mind if he does destroy them (though I doubt if his right arm is strong

116

enough to tear out the thick pages) because the albums are full of ghosts, and even my own ghost is malicious sometimes and begins to haunt me, and it might be much better if all the ghosts were thrown away and I held them only in my head, just as I hold your ghost, Sister Benedicta, knowing that my memory is blurred and feeble and one day I shall look there for the ghosts and find them gone.

DECEMBER 30

I saw a nun today on the tube. Her feet inside the black lace-up shoes looked pinched, as if she was a child of poor parents who couldn't afford new shoes and had told her: "You'll have to make do." Perhaps her feet really were hurting her, because she looked very cross and unable to stop her nun's heart from spilling over with irritation, thinking, why am I here on a freezing December morning with the sacrifice of my life pressing on my toes? Why am I being jolted across London with the stares of unbelievers and their turned backs showing me no gratitude for my years of selflessness and my winters of light-weight clothing?

I stared at her face and pale eyes that had never worn a trace of make-up even when she was young, and wondered what God ever said to her now that her life was half-way gone and the stink of God's world crawled up her nostrils. Perhaps she had been born on Valentia Island and christened Mary and never a day passed without her remembering Ireland, where even the sea was Catholic and God lay curled in the miracle of a pink cowrie shell.

The nun got off the tube at Charing Cross station. She carried a black hold-all. Off to relatives in Kent to celebrate a new year of obedience? Not liking the relatives in Kent with their cosy hearths and their warm tweed suits, wanting only to be back with the Sisters, wherever they were, waking in the six o'clock darkness to start each day with a blessing and a sip of Jesus at her throat.

"We don't really look forward to the school holidays," you told me once, Sister. "We miss the girls." And of course this was so, because the girls, with their high, English voices, kept out the sound of India that you knew would never go away, but was always there, just outside the gate, and what could you do to keep it out when there were so few of you and India was so vast, it sometimes seemed as if it filled the globe and that

118

England had long ago been buried beneath it. "No, we don't look forward to the holidays!" I didn't either, Sister. My house was full of the belly-laughs of soldiers and there was no peace in it.

I saw the nun on my way to the London Library with Leon's London Library ticket in my handbag and an idea in my mind that I would go there and look for a little book about India that might tell me something about the way it is now and what has happened there in the thirty years since the last British soldiers passed through the Gateway of India on to their waiting ship.

I don't go to the London Library very often and in consequence forget my way around its metal gangways and have to keep asking where things are and this infuriates the staff who are used to writers and professors like A. J. P. Taylor who knows the Library as if it were the lines on the back of his hand and never asks for anything. For me, it's a bit like playing "Hunt the thimble" with no one to shout "cold" or "warm" or "boiling!" and I feel like walking out again without a book, except that I'm afraid to walk out without a book in case the staff believe I've stolen one and put it in my handbag. I wander on, guided by numbers and categories, and when at last I came to a section which said "History – oriental" I saw at once that there are no small books about India, only very thick ones, and I felt very glad that I hadn't asked for a small book at the desk, when of course the complexity of India could never be compressed or ignored and all who write about India do so at great length and I should have been prepared for this.

On my way home, on an empty, middle of the morning tube, I started the one book I eventually selected (the smallest in the section, but I'll come back and get a bigger one next time) and it began with an extract from a speech made by the Finance Minister of Congress on 4th August 1975. "The topmost people in India today," he said, "can have any number of servants; two servants in the kitchen and another two servants in the drawing-room," and I thought of our four servants and the way

119

they kept us in idleness for a pittance and can't help but feel there is a connection and that although we are long gone, some of our ways linger on and where on earth are the head and heart of India if this can happen? We hear about the poor, the millions of them, landless, poorly clothed, starving. Photographers take pictures of them; the pictures win prizes at photographic exhibitions. But we don't hear about these "topmost people" with their servants, and I wonder who they are? I shall try to read my library book carefully so that I understand who they are and what they're doing in big houses with servants, building walls round their houses, just as we did, to keep out the beggars at their gates.

London has been very silent today, waiting perhaps for the last day of the year to come and go and the new year to begin. Or maybe I just haven't noticed London because I've been thinking about India and been wearied, as the day went on, by the notion that there is a beggar at the gate of every person and only those who have nothing are quite free of them. In my imaginings, Sister, the beggars change shape: deaf old girl in pre-war tenement doesn't hear the popping of her gas fire, doesn't know her shilling's run out till she looks round and the room is like ice and all her shillings are gone; grubby child dressed in gypsy rags sells dry heather wrapped in foil up and down Knightsbridge, pushes the heather almost up the noses of the powdered women who walk there with crocodile handbags and they don't buy the heather; two Pakistani boys prop up their badly-made Guy and ask for 10p though it's not even November yet, and "Who was Guy Fawkes?" I ask. "Some old geezer," they say and I pass on without opening my bag and I hear them ask everyone who passes – "10p for the Guy!", all the rush hour people scuttling home in suits, "10p for the Guy, sir, please?"

I was too full of my thoughts about beggars to risk seeing Leon, who has spent his life running away from being poor and sees poor people only as reminders of Liverpool in the 1930s

120

and Grandma Constad's bleak little house in Stokeley Street that was one of the worst streets in the city and you could hear the rats squeaking in the dark and "thank heavens they came along one day and said they were pulling it down". Leon's eyes have a membrane that closes at the least manifestation of poverty. Even Christine, with her army surplus coat, was poor enough to wake up Leon's unease, and Evelyn Wainwright was much too poor for him to take on – though in the Fleet Street gym days he had some poor clients and I can't imagine now how he was able to bear them and the terrible waiting he had to endure before he was rich and could snatch his mother away from her high-rise flat, put her into a little dressed-up Chelsea house and forget that he had ever breathed the Liverpool air.

I had planned to take along the first of the albums today. Instead, I forgot all about Leon, letting the day pass without a visit to the nursing home or the Oratory.

Towards evening, I began once again to wonder about Noel and to wish he would send me a card, because his silence has begun to terrify me and I wonder if I shouldn't go rushing across France in search of him, leaving Leon to mend without me. Perhaps he's planning to be silent for ever, and we shall never know, even when we're very old, what became of him after he took Alexandra to the sleeper for Boulogne. "Didn't he leave a *poste restante*?" I asked Alexandra when she came back, but she laughed and said: "Noel never rests! He's probably halfway across the world by now with his whore." I can't picture this "whore" of Noel's. Alexandra never described her. All I know is that he found her at the beach café.

The sun had shone ever since Noel and Alexandra had arrived in Nice in early July and put Alexandra's mini on the ferry for Ajaccio. They found a room at the Hotel des Etrangers in a quiet street in the heart of the old town, telling the patronne they would stay until their money ran out – for a month at least.

"We felt so glad to be abroad," Alexandra told me, "because nobody knew us. And at Easter, when Noel came to

121

stay with me, he'd been worried all the time that someone might find out and write to you. He wanted to go and see Sue and make her swear never to tell a soul, but I stopped him. I knew Sue was still unhappy; she didn't want to see Noel again."

Ajaccio, once a quiet stone-built harbour town, has sprawled back over the hills behind it and the old town is dwarfed by the new, the big hotels and apartment blocks. Leon and I went there once on a co-respondent's yacht, and I found it a restless, noisy place after the quiet bays our gleaming yacht had discovered on the west coast of the island. When I think of Corsica, I never give Ajaccio a glance, and remember only the clarity of the water and the relentless cicada music that goes on day and night in the pines and on the dry, scented hills, and it seems rather strange to me that Alexandra and Noel should have decided to play out their love there, in a quiet old street, when they might have moved on up the coast and found that the sea occasionally crept into little coves where hardly anyone came and where the sand was white.

Alexandra had told Leon and me that she was going abroad with Sue; Noel had informed us he was going to stay with Trevor, who shared his digs at Mrs Walton's, and that they might go off to France or Italy at some time during the vac. Leon and I had a dusty fortnight in Malta at the end of July and tried not to think that Christmas and Easter had come and gone and now the summer was gently passing and in all that time our children hadn't been home.

One morning, on our Maltese balcony, as Leon sat and watched the hot day begin, he said to me ominously: "I think something's wrong." And when we returned to London, he telephoned Mrs Walton to ask for Trevor's number. He rang this at once and Trevor answered and said: "Noel? I don't know where he is. I haven't seen him since the end of term." So that all through August and the first week of September, when Alexandra came home, Leon fretted, just as he had done at Christmas, and nothing I could say was of any comfort to him.

I remembered how I had lied to my mother, lied about my visits to the Reiter's house, lied about my loathing of my grandmother, lied about my meeting with Leon, until I knew I loved him and couldn't lie any more. But I lied in the belief that my mother, being the insubstantial person she was, had no automatic right to the truth: I blamed her for my lying, not myself. And when I found out that Noel was lying to me, I began to ask myself, what have I done to deserve his lying? I lay awake beside Leon, asking the question, asking and asking, but knowing the answer, pretending that I didn't know it, pretending that in all his years I had given Noel my love and knowing really that it was a beggarly love and not worthy of the truth.

We didn't know then that Alexandra was lying too. She sent us a card from Ajaccio saying: "Sue and I and the mini have made it to Corsica, which we love. Weather is on the postcard. Love, A." And we had no idea that Sue was with her parents in King's Lynn and that Alexandra and Noel made love each night in their rented room in a tree-lined backstreet of Ajaccio, and spent their days on the beach with their bottle of wine and olives and cold meat for a picnic, going now and then to drink Coke or beer at the beach café, the café where Noel found the girl.

They stayed on in Ajaccio. In August, the beaches were very crowded, but they didn't mind, rather enjoyed the jostling for places and sunshades, became friendly with some of the people they met on the beach every day, and only occasionally got in the mini and drove the winding route up the west coast of the island, finding on the way some of the little bays Leon and I had swum to from our yacht, stopping there to swim or go in search of a village café, sit there the whole morning, watching the young people go by on their mopeds in the patterning of plane leaves on a white square. They were as brown as berries. They felt that because they had been there a month now, they had taken shallow root in Corsica's hard summer earth and no one would move them until autumn came.

"Our room in the hotel grew so familiar," Alexandra said,

"that I began to think of it as home. I thought we might stay on and on there, because I couldn't imagine ever leaving. I told Madame Gilbertini we'd stay till the season was over, and she changed all her bookings around so that we could keep our room. We wanted to keep *that* room because we belonged in it. I felt it was ours."

In the second week of August, Alexandra cabled Leon for some money. "Damage to mini," her telegram read, "need £100 urgently." Leon sent the money and with it a letter saying didn't Alexandra think it was only fair to spend a little time with us in London before term began and she went back to the cottage? Alexandra didn't reply to this, only sent another cable saying the money had arrived safely.

Alexandra didn't need the money for the car. She wanted to stay on a bit longer at the Hotel des Etrangers and Noel had begun to say their money was running low and hadn't they better think of going back to England? Alexandra took fright. How could Noel suggest this, when she only had to look at their bodies to know that they had been transformed by the sunshine? How could he think of waking and looking out anywhere but through their wistaria-covered window in the room that had held their secret safe for so long? She began to accuse Noel: "You're tired of me. You're ashamed of it all in your heart."

She sent Leon the cable, hoping that once they had money again, Noel would forget his talk of going back. The thought that Noel's love was shallow and would pass made her cry silently in the hot nights while he slept. Surely he would love her as long as they stayed in that room, heard the tom-cats fight in the dark and woke each day to the threads of sunlight coming through the shutters? She was afraid of England with its end-of-summer gales and the routine of its year. Even the cottage became a dread: Noel will leave me there and never come to see me and that will be the end of it all.

When the £100 arrived from Leon, Noel agreed to stay until the first week of September. But sometimes in the mornings

124

now Alexandra would wake to find that Noel had slipped out without a sound. He would come back long after she'd eaten her breakfast and got ready for the day. He told her he'd gone for a walk or had a coffee down at the harbour, watched a big yacht come in.

In Corsica there is a saying that after Napoleon's birthday on August 15th, the weather breaks. The town that gave the Emperor to the world celebrates with parades and feasting and then goes oddly silent, waiting for the rain. Often it rains for two weeks and the old city is awash with floating garbage and the smell of limp flowers, which was how it was when Leon and I got off our yacht, so that I've never seen it in sunlight. True to its custom, it began to rain on the day Leon's money arrived, and the rain kept on for ten days, and Noel said again and again: "I don't know why we decided to stay on. We might as well be in England." But the rain didn't put him off his morning walks, and the nights had a habit of uncovering a skyful of stars, so that Madame Gilbertini would nod at them from her desk and say: "*Vous voyez, il fera beau demain!*"

Then one morning it was fine and hot again. "You couldn't imagine it had rained for ten days," Alexandra said, "the whole town was dry in a few hours, even the café awnings and the public benches." But when she and Noel got down to the beach, they noticed a big crowd at the water's edge and saw when they came near that the storms had washed up a dead porpoise. Its lumpish blue-grey body, coated with wet sand, looked ugly and immovable in the midst of the raffia beach mats and the sunshades and Alexandra didn't want to be there on the beach until it had been taken away.

She and Noel got in the car and drove north-east out of the town towards Vizzavona. The road winds steeply up; wild rosemary grows among the *maquis* of those hard hillsides and the air, buzzing with cicada sound, is a balm. I know the winding road to Vizzavona; there is a good restaurant in the little hill town, and Leon's co-respondent who was always in

125

pursuit of good restaurants, hired a car in Ajaccio and drove us all up there for lunch. I enjoyed the drive more than the lunch. I asked the co-respondent (who was called Walter J. King and was president of his local Wine and Food Society back home in California) to stop the car so that I could walk for a few minues in the sunshine that had eluded us in Ajaccio, but up here was giving an extraordinary shimmering light to the hills. I can imagine Alexandra and Noel on that road, stopping perhaps where I stopped and then discovering that sixty feet below them ran a clear stream and deciding to scramble down to it and bathe because they were hot in the small car and Alexandra felt full of joy and hope again, now that the rain had gone. They drank their bottle of wine by the stream, and Alexandra wanted to stay there all day with Noel until the sun went down. But Noel said no, if they were going to Vizzavona, they ought to be on their way. Alexandra lay still and waited. She wanted Noel to change his mind. "We hadn't loved for days," she told me, "and here was a beautiful hidden place. I waited for Noel to touch me, but he didn't. He pulled me up and we drove to Vizzavona in silence."

In Vizzavona, they sat on a white wall and listened to the church bells. It was a wedding day and the whole town had stopped to marvel. In the cafés, some of the men wore suits with bits of fern and flowers in their buttonholes; their glasses were filled and refilled with pastis before they got up noisily and made their way to the church. "We sat on our wall and thought the bride might come by," said Alexandra, "but she went another way and we never saw her and then the church bells stopped and the cafés were empty and we felt left out."

When they arrived back at the Hotel des Etrangers, Alexandra was tired after the hot, empty day, lay down in the shuttered room and went to sleep. She woke at nine and it was dark and there was no sign of Noel. "I was very hungry," she told me, "but I didn't want to sit in a restaurant on my own, so I decided to go down to the beach café, which played records in

126

the evening and sold pizza. I couldn't find the car. I suppose Noel had taken it, so I walked. The beach seemed a long way off in the dark."

When Alexandra got to the beach, she saw that a group of boys had poured petrol over the dead porpoise and were burning it. Oily flames flared up at the water's edge; the burning flesh smelt of charred salt. But the fire, reflected in the sea, seemed to light up the whole beach, and it was in the light of the burning porpoise that Alexandra saw Noel walking away from her along the beach with his arm round the girl who sold pizza at the beach café. Alexandra stood still and watched her. She wanted to believe that it wasn't Noel's arm that held her. She followed. She heard Noel laugh and the girl from the beach café laughed and then the two of them began to run, hand in hand, on and on along the beach, racing into the joy of being together and laughing at the world left behind.

Alexandra walked very slowly back to the room at the Hotel des Etrangers. Madame Gilbertini smiled at her as she handed her the key. Alexandra took the smile with her to the room, knowing it only needed a smile to release in her the inevitable tears, thinking as she cried, I should have been crying and crying ever since the day I first touched Noel. Because she had known all along that he had a soldier's heart and would defeat her.

DECEMBER 31

The last day of my long year. I must go to see Leon today, to put the year in its place, to remind him that this is the end of it, and tomorrow we might begin, as I was taught at the Convent School, to make resolutions.

I believe I've already made rather a contradictory resolution, which is to break my habit of obedience to Leon and begin to feel free of him. This doesn't mean that I won't care for him when he comes home. I would do anything for him: I would clean him up and wash him like a baby. But I see, now that I've been without him for a while, that he has been quite free of me all our lives, free to consult his own head and heart, but never mine. And my head and heart have grown so unused to being consulted, so used to being disbelieved, that they have become small and covered themselves and let me go on and on in my confusions, so that my soul is like the soul of Harrods – very small as souls go, and always in pursuit of the unnecessary and the unobtainable.

I have also begun to wonder whether, if I am to discover myself – head, heart and soul – I shouldn't break at once with the illusive God who hides in the silences between thought and action and who never comes, Sister, never once when I've knelt down in the bathroom and prayed with my fists in my eyes, and who never even seems to notice the Faithful in the Oratory, paying the price of a bus ride for a candle, but stands aloof and lets their husbands die and their sons drown and knows He will not be blamed, only that the price of candles will go up as the years go on.

Perhaps it is only that I have lost the habit of loving God, just as I never seemed to get the habit of loving myself. And if I persevered, I might rediscover it and feel His presence like a gleam of light in my skull. I don't know, Sister. Sometimes, when I remember India, I think I only loved God just to please you.

JANUARY 1 1978

I did go to see Leon yesterday, but I had no time to write about this, because the evening with Gerald and Davina was very long and tiring and I have crept exhausted into this new year.

An idiotic little word follows my thoughts: *mudgen*. While I was sitting with Leon yesterday afternoon, he reached for the first of the photograph albums that I had taken him and his chin jutted sideways and his mouth began to make the Chinese gurgling sounds I've heard before, but this time, he wasn't content with them and struggled on, going red behind his eyes, until he came out with it: *mudgen*. He stared at me, waiting for me to understand. I was shocked that he'd made a word and wanted to ring for a nurse. I didn't like the word, didn't know what to do with it. I stared back at Leon and couldn't speak. I wanted to say: "I can't make anything of that, Leon. Don't ask me to try." But when Leon saw that I hadn't understood, I could see him getting very angry and confused and he tried to make another word, one that I'd understand, but after another long struggle with his face, he said it again: *mudgen*.

"Do you mean album, dear?" I asked frantically. "Al-bum. Do you mean that? Because I know there are eight, of course I do, but I couldn't bring them all at once, Leon, they're too heavy."

I waited. Leon shook his head and then began to try yet again to say what he wanted to say, but before the word came out, he lay back and shut his eyes and mouth and more of the tears that he sheds every day now slid down his cheeks and on to his pyjamas. I passed him the slate. ("Write it down, dear!" I heard my grandmother shriek.) He took it crossly and in very strong handwriting put: "Noel", underlined it three times and handed it back to me. I looked at it and sighed. I took a breath before I said: "I've told you all this before, Leon, only you don't remember things, dear, do you? I've told you, I don't know where Noel is. If I did, I'd bring him here just as you asked me.

Alexandra left him in Avignon when she got on the train and came home. She left him her mini, but she didn't know where he was going or what he was going to do. He had very little money, so I expected – we expected, don't you remember? – to get a cable, but no cable's come. Sometimes I think I ought to ring up Interpol, Leon, though how you go about ringing them up I honestly don't know, and perhaps even if they made a global search for Noel they might just miss him. He could be in a room in Avignon waiting for something to turn up, or he could be a waiter or a road cleaner or selling the *Herald Tribune* in the square of the Palais des Papes, though heaven knows if any Americans go to France in the winter when it can be so very cold."

I felt so angry with Leon for all this questioning about Noel that I found I was shouting at him. I wanted to cry. I wanted to shout: "You think you're the only one in pain, Leon, but my days are almost as empty of life as yours and I have to keep going for you all, up and down the freezing London streets day after day, backwards and forwards, to hold your hand and pray for you and try to be strong enough to help you all in case you all come back to me – just in case." But I'm glad now that I didn't let my wave of self-pity go tumbling down on Leon. He has begun to try very hard at what Matron calls rehabilitation and this is brave of him and I must keep saying to myself, "he's doing his best", and try not to mind that he can't manufacture a real word, try to forget that when he said *mudgen*, it sounded like an obscenity.

I was glad to get away from the nursing home. Last night I dreamed I saw a pale crab creeping out of the sea at sunset; the sun on the water was beautiful and I thought, here at last is God's gentle world, silent and perfect. But the crab began skittering on the grey sand as the sun fell lower, and I moved further and further from the water's edge, hating the crab moving like a spider, aware that my feet were bare in the sand and that the crab was following my feet. I ran, and the crab skittered after me. The sun went down behind the sea and in the grey light the crab became invisible, invisible but near, and I thought, if only I had worn shoes I wouldn't be so afraid, if only I had decided to protect myself . . .

When I woke, it seemed very clear to me that I had been running from Leon and the hideous faces he makes and that far from wanting to care for him with my own hands, I don't even want to be near him. I'm terribly afraid of these feelings. My only hope is that I shall shake them off and replace them with love and compassion of the kind Jesus felt for the lumbering dumb cripples who hobbled up the Mount of Olives for a touch of His robe. Or perhaps last night Gerald's rum punch was flowing through me like a lie and my heart wasn't really talking.

Gerald had made an enormous bowl of punch, set fruit swimming in it like flotsam and called it "my own invention, Ruby, very alcoholic". And the five of us there – Gerald, Davina, the Hazlehursts and myself – kept raising our silver-plated goblets to toast the slow arrival of 1978, until at last a tired midnight came and Gerald kissed Davina on the mouth and I wanted to say "that's that, then" and drive home. But the announcement of the New Year released in Gerald a very uncharacteristic urge to make a speech, all through which George and Betty Hazlehurst stared at the carpet and Davina did tentative battle with a purple paper hat that kept slipping over her face. I watched Gerald's eyes darting about in search of the goodwill he wanted us all to feel. "I can honestly say," he declared, "that I feel this year to be *New*! I don't expect any of you to understand the extent to which my wonderful Davina has changed my outlook on life; I can only tell you that she is the most wonderful, patient girl I've ever met and that I shall be a very, very proud man the day she becomes Mrs Tibbs."

I couldn't help feeling that it was the rum punch that had enabled Gerald to refer to Davina as a girl, and that when his eyes are seeing clearly, they can't fail to miss the signs of her unspoken journey towards fifty. She is a sandy-coloured person

131

with grey eyes awash in a face that doesn't often smile. She talks as if she was balancing a china teacup in her hands; she has walked her way through a childless life on fragile legs in heavy shoes. As I watched her little mouth open for Gerald's kiss, I thought, she is a strange object for passion – even for Gerald's rather English and unpassionate passion – but at least this probably makes her safe from Italians and perhaps this is the most important thing, because, whatever happens, we must pray that Gerald stays in one piece now that he's so completely mended.

"Are you completely mended?" I whispered to him when Davina was out of the room, but he turned his reddening eyes on me like firebrands and said accusingly: "Davina doesn't like it talked of!" and wandered away from me. And I know now that Gerald will spend the rest of his life pretending that he never loved Sarah and that Davina is no more than the angel of his forgetting.

I wondered if Gerald had told Davina about his ride on my roundabout of a body, because it was very clear to me all through the evening that Davina didn't want to look at me or come near me and was wishing that Gerald had never invited me. She seemed quite happy to stand under the screeching roof of Betty Hazlehurst's voice and didn't jump away at George Hazlehurst's Churchillian growling, but she hardly spoke to me, only to say: "I didn't make the rum punch, Gerald did. And we got the caterers in to do the food, because I'm not used to cooking for a party." And I thought, this is probably what Gerald likes in her, this uselessness and trepidation, and when he holds her, he knows he is holding a child who will remain a child for ever and stay in the shelter of his arm.

I had thought Gerald's teenage children might be there at the party, but there was no sign nor mention of them and I didn't dare ask him where they were in case, after paying for all that expensive hot chocolate in Austria, he'd decided to pack them off to Milan. If I was them, I think I'd rather be in Italy with a brown step-father, and a mother learning to do home-made ravioli, than waking every day to Davina's timid eyes and the thump of her shoes like club feet. But perhaps they were still there in the house in Kensington and had merely gone to a New Year's party of their own, wearing satin vests and with their hair frizzed. Teenage children seem to come and go from their homes like cats – or so the Smiths, who have teenage nephews and nieces, once said to me on the stairs – and have lost all sense of night and day and sometimes I feel rather relieved that I don't know any of them, because on the whole they look rather cruel.

There were some inquiries about Leon from the Hazle-hurst's at Gerald's party, and it was after these that I left. I found that all the questioning about Leon, combined with the punch, made my head ache and I longed to lie down and give no thought to Gerald or Davina or Gerald's children, or indeed to Leon or Noel or Alexandra, because it seemed to me, Sister, as I drove unsteadily home, that each year becomes another, becomes five, becomes twenty, and I have listened as patiently as I can to the noises of these people, but the noises are familiar and as sad as the dry leaves that blew down the corridors of the empty Convent School. Around them all is a high wall that allows no glimpse of a "beyond". The wall has told me there is no "beyond". But I am tired to death of the noises, Sister, and tired to death of the wall.

I read my library book for a while when I got home. I read that half the population of India earns less than £3 a month and that with this they can buy "one egg or two tomatoes or a little boiled millet" each day. I wonder how, with only this in their bellies, they can work from dawn to dusk in the fields under the hot sun that I remember?

JANUARY 2 1978

The Oratory has gone very quiet now that Christmas is over. I went in there today to mutter something for Leon. I don't know what I muttered. Nothing much. I leant on the hard pew and pictured Leon's face struggling, not with a word that wouldn't shape itself, but with the anger that invaded him when Alexandra rang our doorbell late on a Saturday afternoon in September and sat down in front of us and wept. "Where did I fail?" sang out his Jewish heart, "that I have been so betrayed by my own flesh and blood that I have spent my life teaching and working for? You disgust me! I'd rather see rats in a flea-bitten copulation than contemplate your degradation and greed! You've *eaten* each other. Wasn't there anything better to eat, Alexandra, than your own brother?"

"I love Noel. I love Noel," was all Alexandra could say and she repeated this over and over again as Leon's anger flooded her and the tears ran down her face.

"Don't imagine," he shrieked, "that your mother or I will ever forget what you've done to this family as long as we live! You've pulled this family apart and thrown it into a stinking garbage pit. You've murdered this family and don't fool yourself that it can ever, *ever* be reborn. Murdered bodies are dead and stay dead and the stinking rotten earth pushes out its maggots to creep into their mouths, and that's what you've given us all – decay and filth and a mouthful of worms!"

I closed my eyes and pressed my fists into them, wanting to forget that I'd ever seen or heard Leon's anger. But my picture of him and of Alexandra with her tears and her endlessly repeated "I love Noel", slipped not away, only out of focus, so that I saw Leon indistinctly and couldn't recall another word in the torrent of words that came out of him that day, but heard him shout: "mudgen! mudgen! *mudgen*!" to Alexandra and then to me, and to make him stop I began a desperate whisper: "Quiet, Leon! Matron says . . . This is a church – *my* church when I was a girl and in love with a nun. You must be good and quiet and not say that word any more, Matron says . . ."

I looked around the Oratory and saw that it was completely empty. Usually, I keep company there with the unheard whispers of Catholics whose knees are utterly obedient to their genuflections and their hearts and minds to their prayers – or so they seem. Now, I was quite alone. I looked up at the roof and then towards the altar, still covered in its red and gold cloth and I thought of Godmother Louise being carried down her stairs in a red ambulance blanket by Max Reiter, who wouldn't let the ambulance men touch her, he said. I stood in the hall as Louise passed me with her thin face, red-blanketed to the chin, resting against Max's shoulder and she winked at me and whispered: "Don't let the priests near me, Ruby. OK?"

She died the same afternoon, as if the journey to the hospital that both she and Max had put off for so long had quite exhausted her, and as far as I know, Max was the only guardian of her soul as it slipped away from her. Louise saw the Catholic church, with all its rules and punishments, as a school. "I grew out of it," she often said. "God's no better than a headmaster, with his apostles as prefects."

I stared for a long time at the red-covered altar. I had come to the Oratory to ask for strength to help Leon and to try to fill my heart with love for him, Sister, so that I won't feel disgust if he keeps on saying *mudgen*, even when he's home and there's no nurse to come running. But the strength doesn't seem to come; and I don't think God was in the Oratory today. He'd gone to wherever the faithful had gathered. I lit a candle nevertheless. Just in case.

When I came out of the Oratory, it had begun to snow, and I walked home letting the snow fall on me, rather liking it, despite the cold, thinking somewhere in the back of my mind, it'll be falling fast on Norfolk, covering up railway lines.

As I turned the corner into our street, I saw a dormobile parked outside the entrance to the flat, and a young bearded

135

American, wearing an anorak with badges all over it, jumped out of the dormobile as soon as he saw me going in and said: "Pardon me. I'm waiting here for Mrs Constad, and I didn't know if you mightn't be she?" and this all sounded so polite and strange and so absolutely a part of Philadelphia or Oregon or thousands of places where I've never been that I stared amazed at the man, forgetting to reply. When at last I admitted to being Mrs Constad, he looked very relieved and told me he'd been waiting for an hour and would he be disturbing me if he came in out of the snow because he was a friend of Noel's.

He was called Al, or "to be more precise", he said, "Alan O. Orkiss, but Alan O. Orkiss isn't a name that travels well and I always tell everyone to scrap the 'O. Orkiss' and just call me Al. You can call me Al, Mrs Constad, for the time I'm bothering you here."

"You're not bothering me," I said, "would you like a martini?"

It was teatime and he looked amazed.

"I don't drink," he said.

"Well, Al . . ." I began very nervously, "if you say you're a friend of Noel's . . . You see I haven't heard from Noel, not since September and his father's very ill and . . ."

"His father's ill?"

"He's *been* ill. He's been very ill and really it's been such a worrying time and just lately I have begun to worry about Noel."

"Noel's OK.

Alan O. Orkiss began to fumble in his anorak pockets. It was the kind of anorak that has pockets all over it, so that if you decide to go canoeing in it and you capsize, you won't lose your front door keys or your pocket calculator and your french letters won't perish. He took out several maps and guides of Europe and a little wad of lavatory paper before he found what he was looking for: it was a letter with my name and address on it written in Noel's handwriting.

"I'd begun to imagine that Noel was dead," I said as I took the letter, "I imagined him drowned."

"No. He's fine."

The letter was very short. It said:

Dear Mum,

In case you've been wondering – I sold the car and lived off that for a while. Thought I'd have to come home then, but the thought of England is a bad one. Lady Luck (or rather American Luck, chance meeting in Paris with Al Orkiss, bearer of this letter) got me a job. Al's father owns a music company in Harrisburg, Pa. and wants to sell electric organs all over Europe. I demonstrate the organs in a department store; more fun in a way than trying to become like Dad and failing, and my French is pretty good now.

I know you'll do your best with Dad's anger, and tell Alex I hope she's working again. Happy Christmas.

Love, Noel

"I thought of him in Avignon," I mumbled, "I had terrible thoughts of him there."

"No."

"I'd like to write to him. I'd like to write now."

"Well, I have no address for Noel, Mrs Constad, not right now. You see, my dad came over to Paris and thought Noel was doing a good job with the organs and he said right away he'd like to fix Noel up with a better apartment. He was living in the dix-huitième and it was a crummy place, no bath. He'll have moved on by now."

"I could write to the shop, couldn't I?"

"Sure."

"Which shop is it? What's the name of it?"

"It's the Bon Marché but I don't have the exact address for it."

"Don't you? Oh dear. Well . . . shall I make some coffee, Alan?"

137

"Al."

"Oh Al, yes. Shall I?"

"Great."

I went into the kitchen and put the kettle on. While I waited for it to boil, I examined for the last time the terrible image I had allowed to nibble at my mind: the slow progress of Noel's body down the green channels of the Rhône, bumping against the age-old bridges of Avignon and moving on silently towards the sea. I put the image away; replaced it with a picture of Noel smiling under his straight shiny hair in a Paris café. I must send out his winter overcoat, I thought.

I carried the coffee into the sitting-room and persuaded Al to take off his anorak. Without it, he looked very thin and I wondered how he could endure the freezing London days, when surely the sun shone in winter in Harrisburg and it might have been nicer to have stayed there and helped his father with the music business. But he was travelling, he said. He never wanted to stop travelling, and only in the dormobile did he ever feel free. He couldn't understand why everyone in the world wasn't moving in camel trains across the globe, "when, Christ, there's only one globe and one life and why sit in one corner and let the dust fall on you?"

"It isn't necessarily dust, Al."

"Yes it is. And anyway travelling isn't difficult," he said earnestly, "everyone imagines it's difficult and painful and that they won't be able to buy their favourite medicines. But it's not difficult. All you need is a little money and some warm clothes and a map."

"It's never been like that for me," I said, "whenever I've travelled with Leon, we've spent hours with his man at Cooks, planning itineraries and learning about rabies and cholera and the state of the tap water. And it's never been a question of 'a little money'. We've always taken wads of it and our Barclay-cards and Diners Clubs, just in case the wads run out. I mean, I simply can't believe you can live on 'a little money' in France for instance, where they look at pounds with such scorn, you might as well be offering them Monopoly money."

Al laughed. "That's just one way of looking at it," he said.

"I've never seen it another way," I admitted. "I mean, even when Leon goes to America where everyone is so hospitable and pays for everything, he always takes hundreds of pounds and he never seems to come home with them."

"Oh it's not difficult to spend and spend, if you believe you're on a 'holiday'. You're bound to spend then. But I don't think about travelling as a holiday, it's just the way I like to live. I pay my way mostly, working in bars or something and then move on. And I never buy air tickets. I go by ship or over land. You don't see anything from fifty thousand feet."

"Where will you end up, Al?" I asked. "You'll go home in the end, won't you?"

"I don't think of 'ending up'. I mean, 'ending up's like dying, man. Why think of that?"

I asked Al where he'd be going next. He said he didn't really know, maybe back to France, "but I'll be at the Black Sea in time for the summer." And I envied him the joy in his eyes and the thin body he took so effortlessly round the world. I found that with Noel's letter safe in my hands and all my nightmares of Avignon gone, I didn't want to talk about Noel. It was enough to know that he was living his life. I don't need him, I thought, and he doesn't need me, unless one day he runs out of money and sends me a cable. So Al drank coffee and I sat watching him, glad that he was Noel's friend and so very unafraid. I asked him to promise that whenever he was in London, he would look me up. "If you're ever short of a place to stay," I said, "you can stay here. It's a big flat – much too big for Leon and me – and I like it when new people arrive."

As he left, with his anorak zipped up, he said: "This thing about Noel's father, shall I tell Noel?"

"Oh no," I said, "there's no need. There was a moment when I thought he wasn't going to pull through, but he's on the mend now, and maybe it's better if Noel doesn't see him for a while – until he's really himself again. The only thing is, if you could ask Noel to send an address? I'm not going to bother him with letters when I know he doesn't want to be bothered. It's only just in case anything should happen . . ."

"Sure. I'll ask him."

"And Al, if you could tell him I'm not angry with him. I was for a while, but I'm not now. I think it's not in my nature."

"Yeah, sure."

When Al had gone, I thought, I should go straight to the hospital and tell Leon that Noel's in Paris and safe and Leon will stop writing "Noel" on the slate. But I had so enjoyed the visit from Al with his tales of travellings, that the smell and sounds of the nursing home seemed more distasteful than they had ever done. And instead of going there, I forgot about Leon and imagined myself bumping across Europe in a dormobile, spending a night on a hillside in Bavaria with a dark German forest like a silent bear for company and a skyful of spring stars over my head; then on through Austria, not stopping to hear Mozart in Vienna or to find Max's grave, but bumping on and on, crossing into Yugoslavia at dawn, following a hay cart down a red brick village where old women in black were up and about, some sweeping, others sitting still on hard wooden chairs in front of their doors, watching the sun climb up and the farm carts pass and sending the children, no bigger than seven or eight, to take the cows to the fields before school began. I imagined stopping in Sarajevo in the late afternoon: unassuming town packing up market stalls, selling fruit where the Archduke was shot in 1914, town in the middle of nowhere, on the road to Lubliana and Rijeka where at last, a day and a half later, in the darkness, I stopped the dormobile on a hillside road, got out among the rocks and blue thistles and heard the sound of the sea . . .

I went to sleep on the drawing-room sofa. I dreamed I was in Leon's room in the nursing home, in his bed and quite alone. I knew that visitors were going to come and see me; I kept my eyes on the door, waiting for it to open, dreading the moment when it opened and someone – Leon? Alexandra? – came in and spoke to me, because only then would I find out if I could make proper words, or just the obscene babblings that Leon makes. I waited and the room got dark and no visitors came. I was afraid to turn on the light, in case the light was some kind of signal that would bring in the visitors. I was afraid to put myself to the test and began to make plans for avoiding it. If the visitors come, I thought, I'll lie right down in the bed and pretend to be asleep, and seeing me asleep, they'll put down the flowers they've brought and tiptoe out and I won't have to say a word.

It was pitch dark when I woke. On the landing outside, I could hear Mrs Smith saying to some long-awaited guest: "Come in, come in. No, You're not late at all!"

JANUARY 17

I haven't said a word to you, Sister, for fifteen days.

But now I can write it: Leon is dead.

I'm not trying it out. It is real.

It has happened. Leon is dead.

Alexandra has been with me. I sent her a telegram and she arrived. Too late. Because even I, when the nursing home telephoned, well, I ran out into Knightsbridge and screamed for a taxi and I told the taxi driver to race like an ambulance with his horn blaring, but even I was too late. Dr Woods was there, wearing glasses. I'd never seen him wear glasses before. Matron was there with her eyes in shadow. "You're too late," they said.

I stared at Dr Woods and Matron, from one to the other. I could hear their two breaths, the repetitious sighs that kept them alive and I thought, Leon is without breath.

"Why?" I said.

Dr Woods took my arm. "We did everything we could," he said, "be assured of that."

"We had very high hopes," Matron said, "we thought, at his age . . ."

He was younger than me. Still forty-eight, two weeks ago when he died. My mother said: "That's a great mistake. As if it wasn't bad enough him being a Jew."

"He's only forty-eight," I said to Matron and Dr Woods and they nodded.

"It's exceedingly rare," said Dr Woods.

"Why did he die?" asked Alexandra, arriving in her duffle coat two days after he was dead.

"That's just it," I said, " 'why him?' I keep on asking."

"No!" she screamed, "What did he die *of*?"

Matron and Dr Woods led me along the corridor to him. When

I see him, I thought, I may let out a wail, as Grandma Constad would have done. But there didn't seem to be any wailing inside me. I looked. The room was bare of flowers, empty and tidy. Me and you, Leon, I thought, but only for a moment longer. I could hear Matron and Dr Woods waiting outside the room. Me and you, Leon, for this one last time. And your face looks so dry, dear, with the stubble coming through. I can't bear to touch it.

JANUARY 19

There was a cup of tea for me in Matron's room. Dr Woods was called away and shook my hand gently.

"Drink the tea, Mrs Constad," said Matron.

I sipped and said: "I'd like to know . . . when you said so much about rehabilitation. I'd like to know . . ."

"Massive secondary stroke," she announced. She announced this as if it was a parade order. I thought, the whole world is crawling with soldiers shouting orders and I have never been free of them, only with Leon when he was twenty and poor and we ran down Primrose Hill with Max Reiter, only then was I free of them.

"Unexpected," Matron said.

JANUARY 20

Where and how was I to bury him, Sister? I believe I wouldn't have minded the wailing of Grandma Constad, someone to take charge. And yet Leon never went near the synagogue, not since the ordeal of the Barmitzvah when he was a boy and living in Liverpool in the wide shadow of Grandma Constad's skirt. I thought of going to the Rabbi and asking: "What shall I do with him?" But I was afraid of the Rabbi, speaking his secret language that I had never bothered to understand.

"Help me," I said to Alexandra.

She is very thin. She wears no make-up. She is frail and unhelpful. On the day of the cremation of Leon's body (the simplest and easiest way, say the undertakers) I ask her: "Are you alone still or is Sue with you?"

"I'm with you," she says.

JANUARY 22

On the way to the cremation, we drive past the Oratory. I remember the soldier's bride and the flickering candles. I remember that, feeling herself becoming very small, Alice tries to remember what the flame of the candle looks like after the candle has been blown out.

"I used to go there most days," I admit to Alexandra.

"Where?"

"In there. The Oratory."

"Why?"

"To pray for Leon. I prayed he wouldn't die."

"I thought you weren't a Catholic. I thought you'd given it up."

We go in the big car in silence. Alexandra has no gloves and her hands are blue with cold. She still wears her duffle coat and a shabby skirt underneath. I imagine her in a warm department store, trying on new clothes. In the communal changing room, her body is the thinnest.

JANUARY 23

I think it's because I sleep for so short a time each night that I can't write for long in the daytime . . .

Four a.m and I haven't slept. The cats have been carrying on somewhere in the cold streets. Better to put on the light and try to write something down – more than a fragment this time.

Evelyn Wainwright called today. She was wearing a black coat and her hair was moulting all over it and inside the black coat, her being was a-shiver and I think it never rests or is still. I made tea. She'd come about Leon, she said, to tell me how sorry . . .

"I don't really want to talk about him, Mrs Wainwright. He's not a part of me any more."

I said this very firmly. I realized that for days and days, I have kept on saying it: "He's not a part of me any more."

"I've lost my own home, or as good as lost it," Evelyn Wainwright whispered into her teacup, "I was forced to take Partridge in the end, younger than my son, you see, younger than Richard and no good."

"He'll do his best for you, Mrs Wainwright."

"His best won't be good enough."

"When does the hearing come up?"

"Tuesday fortnight. I have to appear. I said I didn't want to appear, but Partridge says I must. If I'd had a better solicitor, I wouldn't have had to appear."

"Won't your son change his mind about selling the house?"

"No. Greed and debts, you see, Mrs Constad. He can't understand my feelings, not for one moment. He says there'll be central heating in the new bungalow, and of course I've lived my life without central heating, but I've never complained about this, not so as you could infer I wanted change. Now, if only, you see, your husband hadn't been taken ill. I know I would have been alright with him. He was such a clever man."

Louise came to my rescue. She took my hand and looked at me with her large eyes. "Don't listen to anyone," she counselled, "Leon is clever and kind and he loves you. Don't listen to your mother who's so crumpled up inside, or to your grand-mother, or anyone – listen to your heart! Max and I will come to your wedding. We'll sing and rejoice for you. But if no one in the world rejoiced, no one at all, it wouldn't matter, just as long as you rejoice, Ruby, and know that you're doing what you want to do."

Evelyn Wainwright talked on. She asked me twice if she was disturbing me and I didn't answer. I held Louise's hand. I said to her: "I love Leon. He's changed me and I love him." And then I let myself lean against Louise, who took me in her arms and I could feel her soft hair against my forehead and I wept. Louise didn't move or speak. She held on to me and my tears made a damp patch on her dress. I felt as if I wanted to stay weeping in her arms for ever, until there wasn't a shred of confusion or grief inside me, and I knew she would stay holding me, however long it took. I believe I wept for a long time. When I opened my eyes, the first thing I saw was Evelyn Wainwright's empty teacup on the coffee table and I looked round the room for her, but she had gone.

JANUARY 25

Word has gone out to the co-respondents. I often wake in the night and imagine I hear the telephone ringing and that when I pick up the receiver, I'll hear a click and then a voice saying: "Oh this is Sam Mundy calling from L.A." But it never does ring and I'm really very grateful for this, because I have discovered that it's very hard for me to say Leon's name out loud and I keep praying that a long time will pass before I have to do this again. I can write it down, write it to you, Sister, and not feel the weight of it, the unforgettable weight of that name on my life. But when I say it, all I can remember is that when I uncovered his dead face, I couldn't bear to touch it with my hand, let alone bring my lips near it.

One evening while Alexandra was here and I was lying in bed trying to read, the telephone did ring. It wasn't a co-respondent: it was Sue. I listened to Alexandra talking to her. She told Sue that she felt very ill in London, that she hated being here and wanted to get back to Norfolk. My imaginings of Sue and the cottage came back. I wanted to say to Alexandra: "This is how I imagine it all, the cottage and the hens and Sue – is it right?" But I knew Alexandra didn't want to talk about her life. She has grown thin and tired with the effort of reshaping it, and only when she feels better will she talk to me. I wonder, though, if Sue is just an instrument in her recovery, to be discarded again just as before, when some soldier's footfall sounds outside her door. Or will she stay with Sue, grow old with her, lover and friend?

"I'm quite outside it," I say to myself, "I can do nothing at all, only send her back in a warmer coat." (I didn't even dare to ask her if it was she who came one day to visit Leon in a duffle coat and went home without seeing me.) But then I laugh. After all this time, Sister, after twenty-five years of loving, this is all I have left to give my children – winter coats!

"A fortnight is a long time," Alexandra said to Sue.

She came with me the next day to the nursing home to collect Leon's belongings, such as they were.

"Why on earth did you take him one of the photo albums, Mummy?"

"He asked for it. He wanted them all."

"He couldn't have wanted to see us, not after all that raging."

"He often asked for—"

"Noel?"

"Yes."

"Why?"

"Who can say, dear? Noel seemed to be part of his confusions. He couldn't say 'Noel', of course. He made noises."

"Didn't he say any words at all?"

"Only one. It was a made-up word."

"What was it?"

"I'd rather not say it."

"Why?"

"I don't like hearing it."

"Why?"

"Don't make me say it, Alexandra."

A fortnight is a long time.

JANUARY 27

But then, when Alexandra had gone and I was alone again and Leon's clothes still hung in the wardrobe and his books and papers in the study lie untouched, then I missed her, even though her ways are cold and strange and she is altogether like someone lost.

JANUARY 28

The smell of Leon is in his clothes. I open the cupboard and put my face into his suits and it's as if his body was inside one of them. The smell of him makes me so ashamed that I couldn't go near his dead face. Did I imagine his death was contagious?

JANUARY 29

Such a bad night again, Sister, and the mating cats are like sirens. When the light comes, my eyes are swollen and there is such an ache in my legs, I wonder if I can get out of bed. I am ageing surely, ageing quite out of time. If I see Gerald again, or Betty Hazlehurst, they will say: "Good heavens, Ruby, you've aged out of all proportion . . ."

Out of all proportion to the paper-thin life, led in silence for quite some years now, ever since Leon went away in search of paradise, out of all proportion to these hundreds of pale days is the hurting weight of Leon's death.

I remember at the Convent School, when one of the Sisters died of heat and old age in the middle of the summer term, we were told that there would be "a suitable period of mourning". We stood in silence for a minute each day at the end of morning prayers, thinking of Sister Jordana's soul, but the "suitable period" didn't last very long, and after that we were allowed to forget about her soul and only a few of you remembered it, I suppose, Sister, and sometimes said prayers for it. And if you were here with me now, Sister Benedicta, you might say to me: "Don't let the period of mourning be too long, Ruby. Don't let it be longer than 'suitable'." And we would kneel down together in the bathroom and pray for Leon's Jewish soul side by side, and then one day you would say: "That's enough. Let the dead bury the dead." And you would help me to forget him. You would bundle his suits off to Oxfam and call the removal men to come and take away all his books and papers and his real leather-topped desk, and in your heart you would be saying: "It's a blessed release. Now she is free again to love Jesus."

"Once you have loved," Louise said to me, "you will never again want to be without love." Louise couldn't see that in hundreds of lives, lovelessness slips in silently, almost unnoticed like a stiffening of the joints, and that *wanting* to love is purposeless, like wanting to be a child again and it is very

151

idiotic even to try. Louise kept love like a nutmeg in her palm, kept it safe and warm all her life, took it half-way round the world and still held on to it, and of all the things I loved about Louise, I admired most her safe keeping of her love. At twenty, I thought I could do the same. But I told you Sister, ten years was all I managed, and it is those ten, not all the rest that followed, that press on me now – the years when I smiled in photographs and the Fleet Street gymnasts marched and vaulted and climbed and balanced from dawn to dusk seven days a week. It is those years I would like to be rid of now. The albums are back on their shelf in Leon's study and I never look at them, but my heart echoes with those old years and all the paraphernalia of Leon's life that still lies around me reminds me not of the man who has just died, but of the man I once loved.

This morning I walked past Sheila's house. She keeps it very nicely, with flowers in the window-boxes and newly painted railings. It is Saturday, and I could see Sheila in her kitchen which was yellow in Grandma Constad's day and now looks very changed, thought I didn't dare to stop long enough to see what colour Sheila has painted it, not wanting her to catch sight of me and think, why's she come snooping round, when Leon is dead now and nothing signifies any more? Two streets past the house, and I contemplated going back. I thought of knocking and saying to Sheila: "Help me to remember that for years he hasn't loved me, but has gone on loving you. Tell me how often he came to see you. Did he always come burdened down with love and take you in his arms? Did he tell you that he felt tired when he came back from America? Why do you think he felt so tired? Did he love not just you, Sheila, but lots of girls, five or ten a year in rotation and a new one each night in Beverly Hills?"

But I didn't go back not even to ask Sheila if it was her, the visitor to the nursing home, in a coat like Alexandra's. Only two more days and it will be February.

January 30

The Smiths announced themselves at my door.

"We thought we'd wait a while before we called," they said. "We didn't think you'd want to see anyone for a while. We won't come in. We'd only like to say . . ."

They have never been inside this flat, nor I inside theirs. London neighbours only seem to talk to each other on staircases or in car parks, as if this is all convention allows and the first one to cross a threshold is breaking some inviolate law.

I asked the Smiths to come in and they hesitated, looking worriedly at each other.

"No, really, we won't bother you, Mrs Constad."

"It wouldn't be bothering me. It seems dreadful that you've never been into the flat. But now you're here, I'd love to put a kettle on."

So they came in. They tiptoed, as if there was a child in the flat who mustn't be woken. I sat them down in the drawing-room and went to make coffee for them and I knew that they were sitting very still and in silence. When I took in the coffee, they sipped it in silence until Mrs Smith (who seems to talk more than Mr Smith, according to the snatches of their life I hear on the landing) said: "What we'd really like to say to you, Mrs Constad, is that if ever you feel you need someone – to talk to, perhaps, or for anything at all – we're here."

I nodded.

"I know you are," I said, "I hear some of your comings and goings, just as you hear mine, and sometimes, I admit, it's rather reassuring to hear you. At Christmas, you see, when there was all that fog on the M4, I was awfully worried about you."

The Smiths looked at each other. I could tell they thought this was eccentric of me, inappropriate.

"Oh we were fine," said Mrs Smith with a smile.

"Yes, we were fine," said Mr Smith.

"Christmas in the country is rather nice, isn't it?" I said.

"Well, we prefer it."

"We used to go now and then, when friends invited us. That extraordinary noise that pheasants make!"

"It's been a good year for pheasants," said Mr Smith.

"Has it?" I said. "My grandmother used to love the sound of a shoot. 'Aha!' she used to say, 'the wonderful shooting season! A good hot breakfast and the excitement of the first drive and the ground all covered with frost.' "

"That's it."

"Not that she'd been to a shoot in thirty years, because my grandfather died long before I was born. She just remembered it."

The Smiths were silent again. I dare say their hearts were bursting with condolences they found they couldn't utter, because they were people who didn't utter things easily and lived their lives in cardigans.

There was quite strong sunlight coming through the drawing-room windows, revealing to me that the windows were very grimy and I thought, why hasn't the window cleaner come for so long, when now of all times, I mustn't let everything slip and fall into decay.

"Has the window cleaner been to you lately?" I asked the Smiths, and once again they looked astonished.

"Has he dear?" Mr Smith asked his wife.

"Well, he came just after Christmas. He always comes near Christmas, so that we'll give him something."

"He didn't come to me, and I was just noticing my windows . . ."

"I'll send him round, shall I, the next time he comes to us?"

"Yes, thank you. I don't know why he didn't come to me when he doesn't normally miss a month. It'll be spring soon."

Mr Smith slapped his knee. "That's the right attitude, if I may say Mrs Constad. Think ahead!" Then he hushed his voice to say: "We lost a child, you know. She was five years old. And

154

quite honestly, I didn't know how we were going to get on after that. But we did."

"Of course, we've never forgotten her," added Mrs Smith, "we couldn't really forget her. I mean, one can't, can one? But as Hugh says, life does go on."

I thought of you, Sister, and a thing you once said: "There is great sorrow in the heart of mankind over the death of a child." And I wanted to say to the Smiths that in India children die easily and in great numbers because of the fly-borne and water-borne diseases that still crawl round the sub-continent, and in the great days of Anglo-India, hundreds of parents of white children sent them back to England and never saw them for months or years on end, because their fear that the children would die was so great. I was never sent back to England, though there was some whispered talk of putting me on a boat for Wiltshire, and I'm glad that I stayed in India and went to the Convent School, even if that was all I really knew of India – the high white wall that never changed colour with the seasons.

"We must be going," said Mr Smith, and they both stood up together and thanked me for the coffee.

"But do remember," said Mrs Smith, "if ever you feel lonely, there's nearly always one of us here, and what are neighbours for?"

The crocuses are coming up in Hyde Park. I walked there today
in bright sunshine with a bag of scraps for the ducks on the
Serpentine. The nannies look younger than they used to,
otherwise Hyde Park hardly changes, and when you're down by
the water with the noisy ducks you can scarcely hear the traffic
noise. One or two boats were out on this fine day and I thought,
if Noel was with me he'd take my arm roughly and say: "Come
on, Ma! Let's go for a row!" And I would enjoy being out on the
water with Noel's laughter for company.

I have had no word from Noel or from Al Orkiss, who may
never have gone back to Paris after all, and it seems very wrong
to think of Noel in France, not *knowing*, not even suspecting
that something might be wrong. I think I should try sending a
letter to the department store called the Bon Marché, just
putting: Département de Musique, Bon Marché, Paris, and
hope that every postman knows the store as well as the London
postmen know Harrods and there is no need to write a street
name or a zone number, or anything at all by way of direction.

If I wrote to Noel and the letter reached him, he might come
home. But I would have to tell him in the letter that Leon left
him nothing. I put off as long as I could my visit to the solicitors
"concerning the Last Will and Testament of your husband,
which is lodged with us", but when at last I got there, the
document shown to me was very short and simple: Leon has left
me everything he had, and there is no mention of anyone else in
the Will, nothing for the children, nothing for Sheila. And this
was so unexpected that I said to the solicitor: "This can't be
right. He can't have forgotten them!"

And what do I want with all Leon's money earned from the
famous co-respondents, fifteen guineas an hour for his innate
understanding of the law and the thousands of invisible words
that poured out of him year after year? All my life, I have been

left sums of money – from my mother, from my grandmother whom I couldn't bear to be near, even from Louise and Max who had no children to leave it to. I am rich. Riches have made me fat and silent.

FEBRUARY 1

Today I got an invitation to Gerald's wedding. I won't go to it. With the invitation, a note was enclosed (Gerald, in his new happiness, hadn't wanted to ring me).

> *My dear Ruby,*
> *I cannot begin to tell you how shocked I was by the news of Leon's death. Surely, it was little expected and this must be a terrible moment in your life.*
> *Davina so enjoyed meeting you and shares in my heartfelt condolences. If there is anything, anything we can do for you, please do not hesitate to ring.*
> *Yours ever, Gerald.*

If Leon had come home and recovered his speech and stopped all the crying he did in the nursing home, I would have told him, sooner or later, about my sexual voyage with Gerald and we both would have laughed about it, because Leon often said to me in the days when he loved Sheila, "It would do you good, Ruby, to have an affair; I wouldn't mind." But I never did have an affair. There was nobody to have an affair with.

The only other man I've ever longed to love, years ago before I met Leon, was Max Reiter. My loyalty to Louise – I hope – would have made me refuse Max if he had crept up to my cold room one night, and yet I often lay there, at the top of his house, imagining him and Louise in their big bed, imagining in my virgin head how the weight of Max's body would feel on mine, his great rollocking, noisy body, whose smell I breathed ecstatically each time I was near him. But the only time I held Max's head on my shoulder was when he was sitting in his armchair, soundless and dying of heartbreak, and chose one day to reach out for me and weep. The smell of him seemed to have changed by then. He smelled sour and musty, and only the years of my loving him and Louise made me stay close to him.

FEBRUARY 2

I wrote to Noel today. I should have written before, Sister. Tomorrow and it'll be a month since Leon died, and I've made no effort to reach Noel, so that when he gets my letter – if he ever does – he'll say to himself, why did it take her so *long*? I keep re-reading the letter and wondering about it:

Dearest Noel,
> *It was good to learn from your friend, Al, that you're fine and working in Paris. I had worried about you.*
> *At home, Noel, a terrible and unexpected thing has happened. Your father died on January 3rd. He had been ill, darling, since early December when he suffered a severe stroke that paralysed parts of him. He couldn't do anything for himself and couldn't talk properly, but I didn't let you know all this, because the doctors told me he would be well again one day if he was taken care of and none of them thought he would die. I went to see him every day and he did seem to be getting on better at the end of December, so that the day I met Al, I felt confident enough to say to him, don't worry Noel with news of his father's illness, because I thought he'd soon be home and on the road to recovery.*
> *I don't know what to say. This has been such a troubled year, and the loss of Leon is terrible for us all. I believe that he loved me as well as he could and I shall never complain that he might have loved me more. But I know how very, very much he loved and regarded you. Never doubt this. No father could have loved his son more and when he was ill, although he couldn't say your name, he kept writing it down and asking me to bring you to see him, which of course I would have, had I known where you were. Then you could have seen for yourself what happened.*
> *I imagined you in Avignon, I don't know why. I'm glad you're not there and I feel sure you have friends in Paris who will stay with you and let you cry, if you feel like crying. Or if you feel you'd like to come home for a while, here I am, Noel, with no disapproval or*

159

anger left in me, only a feeling that I haven't seen you for a very long time and that I love you and Alex with all my heart.

Please take care of yourself.

Mummy.

P.S. There is nothing for you or Alexandra in Leon's will, but I shall remedy this and let you and Alex have his money, once Death Duties are paid. And if you need a little money now, please write and ask.

P.P.S. This letter is inadequate to tell you what has happened, which is why I put off writing it for so long. I believe I have always mistrusted letters.

My love once more, M.

Only the letter to you, Sister, is important. It is helping me to make sense of my world. Sometimes, I write for most of the day and forget to eat, and when I see myself in Knightsbridge windows, I notice that I am thinner than on the evening we went to the Hazlehurst's dinner party and I wore my mauve cocktail dress. If I were to try it on, I think my mauve dress would need taking in.

FEBRUARY 3

A month today since Leon died. A fortnight since Alexandra went back to Norfolk. My letter to Noel is on an aeroplane. In a few days, I might have word from Noel that he's on his way, or word from Alexandra that the hens are laying again and the crisis of the year is passing, a little each day as her garden begins to push out signs of spring.

But I tell myself I mustn't think of Noel and Alexandra because they are as they are, just as the seats on London buses are of a certain size and shape and no amount of wailing and noise can change them, so that all the noise and wailing are utterly pointless and it is much better to endure the bus ride in silence, not giving a thought to the seats, glad to be on a bus, going somewhere.

When I'm not writing this letter, I read my library book. I read about a dawn on the outskirts of New Delhi, a grey city dawn on the grey rags of an old man, the stick-boned body of all India's poor, wakening to a terrible new day with a ravening stomach and a heart scarred by lack of hope. In the city centre, a boy in clean white socks rides in a rickshaw to school with a sterilized-water bottle and a packed lunch. The boy's blue-black hair gleams with health as the sun comes up.

I wonder if, now that Leon's dead, I can go on using his London Library ticket? Because the book I chose is small compared to almost all the other books about India in the shelves there and surely isn't big enough to explain to me why the old man lies in the gutter less than a mile away from the plump child riding in the rickshaw.

My father used to say: "Independence for India is folly! The Hindu mentality is lazy and untrustworthy. The Hindu needs leaders – real men!" And if he was alive in his well-polished boots to see the distress of India today, he would say: "You see! All would have been well, if we'd stayed on. They wouldn't be in this mess!" But I know, and perhaps you would have recog-

161

nized in the end, Sister, that India had grown tired of us and our bossy ways and wanted us gone.

But of course men like my father didn't want to leave when they had been so spoiled and pampered and looked up to, and thought of themselves as superior beings. The War Office was chock-a-block with beings who thought themselves superior, so that in the end, all the superiority cancelled itself out and my father sat at his desk and mourned for his "men" and his white-clad servants, for the days when he was ruler. He mourned for all of this so much, just like Napoleon on St Helena saying: "When I think what I was and what I am now!", that all his boisterousness and shouting went out of him and his hair began to moult and he took to farting in public, a thing he never would have done in his Indian days. My mother didn't seem to notice or care that the boisterousness and shouting had gone, or that his hair was falling out, but the farting, she couldn't bear that, it made her sick, she said, "and when I think," I heard her whispering to my grandmother one evening, "that I'll have to live with those . . . noises for the rest of my life!"

In the end, she didn't have to. Two years after our return from India, cancer of the bowel was diagnosed and my father was sent to the King Edward VII Hospital for Officers. Waiting to die, he had only this to say: "It was sitting on my bum that killed me! I'd have been alright if they'd let me stay on in India."

For all my physical likeness to him, I never felt close to him and I never mourned him. "He's an amiable buffoon," Louise once said and that is how I have always thought of him, shouting and yet saying nothing, telling jokes – "not in front of the ladies, eh Rutherford!" – clowning and belly-laughing and now and again slapping a wet kiss on my cheek. I have lived my life quite happily without him. I shall go on remembering him now and then, but I never think of him with sadness. I'm glad that he and my mother aren't alive now to meddle with my confusion. A cold wind sighs over their Wiltshire graves and I keep away.

FEBRUARY 4

I got on a Number 11 bus and went to Fleet Street today. I wanted to see if the gym and Leon's old office were still there in their alleyway.

The building is there, with its metal windows and air of neglect, but its use has changed. It belongs now to the Inner London Education Authority and is a centre for extraordinarily divergent things like Yoga and Accountancy. The room that was Leon's office is presumably a classroom where foreign students can learn English and English students can learn foreign languages and Urban Planning and underneath them in the old gym, people come and go for Yoga and Judo and Flower Arranging. I stood for a while on the very spot where I used to wait for Leon, just inside the door, and read the long list of activities that went on there. I felt rather glad that no young, ambitious solicitor sat working away in Leon's room and that the building was so productive and lively, and I realized of course that this was why I had come: I wanted to see and feel change.

I felt sprightly on the bus home. I held the thought of the changed building in my head and it cheered me up.

I haven't been near the Oratory for days. I've begun to feel that I may never go in it again, that I have given it back to those who use it rightly. "You must remember this, Ruby," you once said, Sister, "we must not go to God only when we are in trouble. God is not a government department." And I know that you were right: this is not the Catholic way. But I'm not a Catholic any more, Sister. I've forgotten how to be one. In the Oratory, I always felt like a stranger and, worse than this, I always doubted. And the ghost of Louise with her whispered "Don't let the priests come near me, Ruby," laughed at my conversations with God. "What an odd way to try and save Leon!" she kept saying.

And I think I knew that in the end Louise would win. Only if God had given me some sign, by saving Leon, might I have kept going on my journey back towards Faith. "But God seldom gives signs, Ruby. It is wrong of us ever to seek for signs." And the truth is that I never found God in the Oratory. He never heard me.

FEBRUARY 6

Still no word from Noel. I imagine my letter on the five o'clock mail into the Gard du Nord, dumped on a metal trolley in a sack, this one sack forgotten. For surely if Noel had received it, he would have written straight away. He would have taken the day off, gone back to his room or walked around Paris and thought about Leon, who looked at his son the day he was born and said: "I see myself." He would have remembered Leon's hopes and boasting, the visit to Cambridge, the big carpeted office "that will be yours when you qualify for it, Noel", and the tight little family we once were when we spent holidays in Wales and Leon played football with Noel on Harlech beach. And he would have wondered as he lay there or walked whether this death, coming quite soon after his loving of Alexandra, wasn't his responsibility in some way, for he could only guess at what had happened after he put Alexandra on the train. He'd had no word from us and asked for none. He hoped we'd forgive him, perhaps, and that Leon, whose plans for him had been so ambitious with talks of partnerships and big salaries, had simply been wise enough to say to himself, "Plans are foolish and I should never have made them. I've only myself to blame."

Perhaps, if Al is back in Paris, Noel will take a holiday from selling organs at the Bon Marché and he and Al will drive home to England on Harrisburg money and my life will suddenly become busy again, cooking proper meals and ironing jeans. If they do arrive, I think I shall ask Al if I can go for a ride in the dormobile.

FEBRUARY 7

I went through Leon's cupboards. I threw away some old, frayed shirts and all his underpants, but folded his other clothes, set them out on the bed, and made them into brown paper parcels to take to the Oxfam depot. All the things he'd had with him in the nursing home I threw away, and then I washed out all his cupboards and drawers, just as I would have done if the flat had been sold and I was leaving everything ship-shape for the new tenant. Only his study I don't dare touch. It surely contains the folded corners of other people's lives and I daren't disturb these.

I went straight down to Pimlico in a taxi with the Oxfam parcels and left them with an arthritic woman who was sorting through hundreds of pairs of shoes. "Some of the shoes in these parcels," I began, indicating Leon's, "have hardly been worn . . ."

"Put them there," she snapped, and I hurried out.

The Oxfam depot is so full of discarded clothing that I couldn't blame the arthritic woman if she couldn't stand the sight of another load arriving, especially when so many of the clothes must be so unsuitable for their faraway destinations, and it's hard to imagine earthquake victims in Ethiopia being content to stumble across the rubble of their lives in cocktail dresses.

On the way home, a drizzle set in and I tied a plastic hat over my hair, looking very odd, like an American I suppose, and the wind blew the drizzle on to the backs of my legs and I thought of the snapping woman going through Leon's nicely-made suits and saying to herself: "Another rich sod with money to burn."

Perhaps I should have taken more time deciding what to do with Leon's clothes. Perhaps I should have waited to see if Noel wanted the cashmere cardigans and the silk ties, the expensive stuff of countless Christmases. Or Sheila? As I waited for a bus at the bottom of Lower Sloane Street, I wondered if in some

166

clumsy way I might not have offered them to her, because Leon hadn't dared to leave her anything, only the house with its painted window-boxes she cared for so meticulously and surely she was expecting something from him after she had given so much?

Then I began to wonder if the Oxfam clothes might not one day find their way to India, where floods and disasters occur more often than in any other country in the world, and an image came to me on the bus of Leon's crocodile shoes floating down the Ganges on the feet of a dead man.

FEBRUARY 8

An airmail letter arrived today from Noel. His handwriting has got much worse, as if he hasn't practised writing at all since he left England, and I could hardly read what he'd put. The letter was quite short:

Dear Mum,

Al told me Dad had been ill. He'd never been ill in his life, had he? so I knew it was something serious. I considered coming back, but honestly I don't feel ready for England yet.

But poor you with all his memories and possessions. If you'd like me to come home for your sake, then of course I will, though I think you'll have to send me the air fare. I'm still stuck with the organs as I can't get a proper work permit, though they say I will in time.

Paris is beginning to get rid of its winter and is a good place to be. I've done no crying for Dad. I don't seem to want to. I'm no good at loving anyone.

I wonder if you'll stay on in the flat? It must be depressing for you and perhaps a move would be best.

I could do with some money really. I can never eat out on what I earn and I'm tired of Al paying for everything. But could you send it yourself and not through Dad's firm or anything. I can't bear the word 'solicitor'. Or come and stay for a few days.

There is a nice hotel on the corner of my street, where I could book you a room.

I think of you,

Noel.

FEBRUARY 9

I have nearly finished my little book about India. This morning I read that the high-caste Indians who own the tea gardens have adopted the style of dress of their British predecessors, the shirt, shorts and knee socks that is like a colonial uniform, and surely they must see how ugly this is? Along the estate roads, the plantation workers live in shacks without electricity or water, and although most of them must be too young to remember the British, those who do remember must look at the high-caste tea bosses and say to themselves: "Everything has changed and yet nothing."

I read of India as a mutilated land. The shirts and shorts of the tea-planters, the self-wounding of the stick and bone beggars on the steps of the tourist temples: here are symbols for a country that is bleeding to death and yet keeps sharpening up the primitive weapons of the past, with its ancient acceptance of privilege and degradation. And each year, the river of the poor rises and goes tumbling into the cities and out along all the roads that lead to the cities and now in New Delhi there is talk of machine guns to keep the river out.

Be glad then, Sister, that your skull rests in some winter churchyard and that your eyes never saw the brown river rise in the hills and come rushing towards the white wall of the Convent. You would have been terrified. You would have remembered what happened in the days of the Mutiny, you would have thought, Mary Mother of God, we'll be clubbed to death by the river, and picked up your grey skirts and run as fast as your nun's shoes could carry you. And when it was all over, you would have asked God why it had to be so, why the wall wasn't high enough to keep out the river, why it couldn't have gone on just as before?

And I've begun at last to think that I've said enough to you, Sister Benedicta. I've imagined that you've sat in your room at sundown, sat with your arms folded as I've talked on and on, your body still, listening patiently. But then, when it got dark, you would have stopped me gently, as you always did and said: "Come back tomorrow, dear, and tell me the rest."

170

FEBRUARY 10

I have asked Partridge, who is quite a clever young man with blond hair (and I don't really know why Evelyn Wainwright had no confidence in him) to look after the question of Leon's money. For years, Leon behaved like a very rich man, but it turns out that his investments are worth only about £40,000, which isn't much by Leon's standards, and I can't help wondering if he didn't give a lot of his money away without my knowing it – to Sheila perhaps or to other women he never told me about, but saw secretly on the evenings he said he was dining with clients and I sat in bed with a library book.

I've signed a lot of papers, making over all Leon's money to Noel and Alexandra. And this morning, I walked to an estate agent in Knightsbridge and put the flat up for sale.

When I look round the flat, I realize that I've never cherished it as a home. I've worried on and off about the lighting or the colour of the curtains, but nothing very joyful has happened in the flat, nothing that I can remember now, and I want to be rid of it. It won't be difficult to sell because it's the kind of place where hundreds of people want to live, almost within sight of Harrods and with quiet neighbours in cardigans to meet occasionally on the stairs.

Partridge seemed to think my decision to sell the flat is very wise. "If I were you, Mrs Constad," he said, "I'd find myself a nice little place in the country, become part of village life." And I nodded at this very obvious wisdom, but I heed no one these days, Sister, I've lost the habit of it. I heed no one but myself.

171

FEBRUARY 11

I went to Highgate again today. The weather was cold and blustery, typical February, and not like the last time I was there, when the sun shone. In its winter briar tangle, leafless except for the climbing ivy, Highgate Cemetery looks neglected and cold and all the graves are sodden. I had no Australian daffodils to throw down for Louise, and her mound looks very colourless, in strange contrast to the way she was, because even in five-star hotels she used to dress in gypsy colours and her favourite thing in the St John's Wood house was a beautiful Persian carpet Max had bought for the dining room, and the colours of this were reflected everywhere in the house – soft blues, ambers and scarlets. At one candlelit Christmas, I remember thinking, the carpet is *the* magic carpet and it has made all our eyes shine.

The cemetery was deserted and I seemed to be the only person there on this chill day. I bent down and touched the writing on Louise's headstone. "I'm on my own now," I whispered.

Then I walked on a bit along the bumpy path, looking at the other graves, but not really noticing them. I thought, thank God you lived, Louise, and showed me a life that was so joyful and unafraid. I so often remember you. You are the nicest memory I have.

April 1

Strange to think I should have chosen this day – April Fool's day, Gerald's wedding day – to go.

There has been no time for writing, Sister, not for days. There has been so much to arrange and put in order, and prospective buyers have been trampling round the flat, dozens of them and each one delighted with the flat's handiness for Harrods. Only to one couple – the first who came – did I say: "I find I don't go there any more," and the woman looked at me as if I was insane and said: "I'd live in Harrods if I could, not just near it." However, this flat seems to be the nearest she could get, and she and her husband have decided to buy the lease which has forty-nine years to run, so perhaps she will grow ancient in the flat and be buried by Harrods' Funeral Department.

"It's very handy for me that you've decided to buy the flat," I told her, "I'm going away, you see, and I want everything to be settled quickly."

"Oh," said the woman, "where are you going?"

"I'm going to India," I said.

I was on my way to the London Library, Sister, when the idea came to me. I was going there to take out another book about India. I wasn't afraid of the Library any more, knowing my way to "History – Oriental" this time. I thought, they won't sneer at me today and wish I was Antonia Fraser.

But just after I got off my bus in Picadilly and began to walk down the Haymarket, I noticed my changed reflection in the plate glass of a travel agent's window and I thought, I'm not the fat woman who once wept in the powder room at Harrods. Fifty-year-old woman with bad deportment and a lot of money, the old self that was so obedient to Leon says: "There's no hope for you, Ruby Constad. Best to stay put, where at least you will die in comfort. Better to stay with what you know and understand, or you will become quite lost, like you were in your dream going to Norfolk." But then I remember Al Orkiss with his dormobile and my imagined journey across Europe and I know that I wasn't afraid then, just as, walking down the Haymarket, I knew that I wasn't at all afraid of going to India.

The idea arrived in me very suddenly and stayed chattering in my head like Punch and Judy noise, so that I could no longer hear the traffic and forgot all about the London Library, walking mechanically right to it and then on past it with my book still under my arm, as a flurry of snow began to fall on London and I knew that I wouldn't stay to see out the winter. I only need a bit of time, just the time it takes to set things in order, I thought, and then I shall be gone. It will be the last – the only – adventure of my life.

I wrote to Alexandra, giving her my date of departure and telling her that she will be getting some money from Partridge. I wrote to Noel and sent him £200 and in both letters I said: "I don't know when I shall be coming back. Whatever I find, however upsetting and frightening, I shall try not to bolt for home. And anyway, with Leon gone and the flat being sold, I need to rethink what 'home' is. People like Al Orkiss seem to have no concept of 'home', and I think I envy them, though of course I wouldn't have said this before."

I waited for the postman this morning, in case there was a reply from Alexandra, but none came. I think I hoped to get her approval of my journey, but she doesn't seem able to give me her attention. My journey isn't important to her. "Do what you like," says her silence, "and let me get on with my life." But I still wonder about your life. Alex. I wonder if you are at peace in your days in the cold garage studio and your nights with Sue who must have forgiven you although you never said she had, and have you got some more hens, dear, to replace those you let die?

Perhaps when I come back – in the summer or in the autumn? – you will start talking to me again, but while I'm travelling I shall try not to think of you.

174

Nor of you, Sister. There will surely be little in India now to remind me of your quietness, your clean room with the raffia blinds. You are gone from India now. You came back to your English convent, and when you died, the Mother Superior announced that there would be "a suitable period of mourning for Sister Benedicta", and when the "suitable period" was over, no one ever thought of you again, with your memories of the Viceroy's pageant and the rains that broke the same day and fell on the Viceroy's plumes. I may have been the only one to think of you, and you have helped me in the way that you always helped me, by your silence.

We have been flying for more than two hours. I saw the sun go down into the clouds and now, underneath me, I can see a city that is no more that a tiny scab of light on the darkness. I'm on my way.